Tadashi Karato

A Tale of the Camellia

Copperplate engraving from "Amoenitates Exoticae"
by courtesy of the Yokohama archives of history, Japan

Tadashi Karato

A Tale of the Camellia
A novel based on historical facts

From Japanese by
Tadashi Karato and Frieda Delvaux

Seijinsha

The author, Tadashi KARATO, was a scholarship holder at the University of Stuttgart and thereafter he obtained a master degree in engineering at the Waseda University of Tokyo. He spent many years professionally in Germany (Düsseldorf) and in London. In Japan he has published six books, of which the most recent is "Sanmen Tsubaki" (Three Sides Camellia).

A Tale of the Camellia.
Copyright © 2024 by Tadashi Karato.
All rights reserved. Printed in Japan.

This book is the English edition of "An'ei no tsubaki", Published in 2012 by Banraisha in Tokyo. Permission for the English translation was obtained from the publisher.

First published in Japan by Seijinsha Inc.
First Japanese Edition: October 2024
10 9 8 7 6 5 4 3 2 1
ISBN 978-4-909299-28-4

Table of Contents

Prescript 7

Prologue *10*

1. Carl Linnaeus *19*
2. Johannes Burman *26*
3. Engelbert Kaempfer *46*
4. Africa *62*
5. Japan *75*
6. Journey to the capital Edo *93*
7. **Whereabouts of the Camellias** *114*

Epilogue *124*

Postscript *128*
References *129*

Prescript

for the English edition of 'A Tale of the Camellia' (An'ei no tsubaki)
Professor Emeritus, Tokai University   Dr. Takayuki Tanaka

I first got in contact with Mr. Karato at the end of 2015, when he applied to attend the International Camellia Congress in Dali, Yunnan Province, China. After he retired from Shimizu Corporation in 2011, where he had worked for nearly 40 years mainly in Europe and other countries, he published "An'ei no Tsubaki" (The Camellia of An'ei).

First of all, I have to mention how surprised I was when I read the book. Though it is a novel (fiction), the description of Carl Peter Thunberg, the Swedish botanist and the main character of the novel with the people around him, made me feel as if I was there in the 18th century. I had been studying on the origin of sasanqua so that I knew Thunberg well as he was the nominator of *Camellia sasanqua* Thunb. the scientific name.

As Karato, however, knows much more than me on the history of the introduction of camellia into Europe, I could not tell the boundary between historical fact and fiction. Then I checked the record of not only Thunberg but also "Amoenitates Exoticae" by Engelbert Kaempfer and the history of Dejima and others to confirm the fact. I could not find mistakes on the historical record in the book as far as I checked. While, I believe Karato is a very special person who can understand deeply both the Japanese and the European cultures and customs at the time.

The first Japanese scientist whom Karato had established a relationship with, was not myself, but the late Dr. Chuji Hiruki, Professor Emeritus of the University of Alberta, Canada, a world authority on plant pathology and the vice president of the International Camellia Society. He also spent his long life abroad and after retirement he started studying on camellia and wrote books about the history of Goto Islands, his hometown in Nagasaki Prefecture, Japan. Thus, Karato and Dr. Hiruki had their passion for Japan and camellia in common, suggesting that it was born from their long life abroad.

Horticulture flourished in Japan during the Edo period (1603-1868) and camellias were the pioneer of the boom. The camellia became very popular among the upper classes in the 17th century, and at the end of the century it spread from the upper classes to the common people and from Kyoto to Edo (Tokyo).

While in Europe, the camellia boom occurred around 1830 during the Edo period before the so-called Japonism which started from the late 19th century, suggesting that the camellia boom was a precursor of the Japonism. In the Edo period, Japan closed itself off politically from the rest of the world. In 1830, more than 700 camellia cultivars had already been bred in France, and more than 100 cultivars in England, Germany, Italy, Belgium, and other European countries, respectively. Although camellia is cold hardy comparing with other evergreen plants, they used to be cultivated as a greenhouse plant in the northern region of Europe. Therefore, only the upper classes could enjoy the camellia with green foliage and gorgeous double-petaled flowers in the winter season, a kind of status symbol. Later, camellias flourished in Spain, Portugal, southern France, Italy, southern Switzerland, southern England, the United States, Australia, New Zealand, and South Africa, where the climate was warmer and camellias could be grown outdoors.

In Portugal, camellia is even also called "Japoneira," which means Japan. The record of camellia cultivation before the camellia boom in around 1830 was not many, though it must have been introduced before.

Engelbert Kaempfer wrote that in Japan there were beautiful evergreen tree ornaments including 23 cultivars of "Tsubaki" (camellia) in the "Amoenitates Exoticae" (1712), but he did not introduce any plants then. It was in 1777 when the first living plants of camellia were introduced to Europe. Maybe, one of the plants should be still alive in the Schloß Pillnitz, Dresden, Germany. Though it was a wild type single flower and later double flower cultivars which originated in Japan were introduced and have played an important role for the breeding in Europe, we must know how they loved the first introduced individual as the plant was taken very good care of for 250 years in the special greenhouse.

This novel treats this very important historical event.

The prologue in which the main character is not Thunberg but the author, Karato himself, and how the camellia in Dresden inspired him to write a book, leads us into the world of this novel. As I wrote before, it was a surprise that the novel is based on historical facts to the extent but merged with fiction.

I met the main character, Thunberg, and his Japanese wife "Hana" with the beautiful romance and sad parting, which reminded me that it was a novel.

Now, Karato has been a director of the International Camellia Society since 2022, and we are collaborating preparing for the 2025 International Camellia Congress in Tokyo. After the German version, this book has now been translated into English and will be presented at the congress. I sincerely hope that this wonderful novel "An'ei no Tsubaki" full of not only camellia love but also the history of the introduction of camellia into Europe, shall be read by camellia enthusiasts.

Prologue

  Lufthansa Flight 711 took off from Narita Airport in Japan and continued smoothly, leaving the Sea of Japan behind and further over Russian territory. The image on the in-seat screen in front of me showed the flight route for the day. The route went to the north which was different from the one through central Siberia that I knew, and it was closer to the Arctic Circle.
I was curious and asked a flight attendant who was passing by, "Why are we flying closer to the Arctic Circle today?"
"I guess it's the wind."
She answered curtly.
I could not help but agree with her, and had a vague hope that if I was lucky, I might be able to see the polar lights.
Luckily, the seat next to mine was empty, which I thought would make the long flight a little easier. The other seats were occupied by mature travelers. From the seat behind me, I overheard an elderly couple talking about their upcoming trip.
The lady asked the man,
"When we get to Frankfurt, where are we headed next?"
"I've told you many times. Madrid."
The husband answered gruffly.
"Oh yes, Germany is too cold to travel there this time of the year, so we've decided to go to a warmer country, haven't we?"
"That's right, we make an early spring trip to Spain and Portugal."
 Listening to this talk, I recalled a conversation I had with my wife who did not accompany me on this trip. I had explained to her in

detail and invited her to go with me. The final conclusion was that she would not go to Germany in winter because it was too cold.

"I'll go alone then."

"By all means. If it's a quest for the German 'camellia legend,' you might as well go alone.

If it were May, I would be happy to join."

"May is too late."

I was free to go on my own without any worries about the future, and I was able to do so without any restrictions.

Speaking of my wife, she must have invited her cake baking friends over to our house by now, and must be having coffee and talking about all sorts of things.

Last autumn, I retired from the company I had worked for during many years and started spending more time at home every day. I have never been bored with organizing my hobby collections or thinking about what I would like to do in the future. The idea of starting something came to me when I was reminded of my wife's daily life, seeing her cheerful and happy.

I was an engineering salaryman working for a construction company. More than half of the time during the nearly 40 years I worked, was related to overseas construction projects. When I was in the engineering department, I often had to leave the head office in Tokyo whenever something happened. It was not uncommon for a single business trip to last up to three months. After retiring from the company, I organized my old documents and when I reviewed my professional memories, I noticed the number of foreign countries I had travelled to, including private trips. To my surprise I found that I had visited 35 countries.

During my working years, I was so busy with work that I did not, or rather could not, give much thought to my family.

Although the children have grown up now, there is no doubt that my wife went through a lot of hardship. Now that I am retired and at home, there is no way I can complain about what she does. In addition to baking cakes, she is enjoying patchwork, flower arrangement, calligraphy, Japanese dancing, and other hobbies together with other women who share her interests. It must be far better for her mental health than spending time alone in the house during her husband's absence.

One day after I retired, I saw an image of camellia blossoms on the TV news and was reminded of 'the legend of the camellia' that I had heard about in Dresden, Germany, when I visited there a long time ago.

It was the beginning of December 1998. I was working on a construction project site in the town of Tychy, a suburb of Katowice in southern Poland. I was invited to go to Dresden by a German friend of mine on business. I did not know what to do with the gloom of Poland's dark winter, so I took a few days off from work and headed out. This time, the friend offered to provide me with a Japanese-speaking guide. This was my second visit to Dresden. So, although I didn't really need it, I was happy to accept the courtesy. The person who showed up was a lady who had studied Japanese at the university. She was the mother of one child, Martina, and she was a kind and pleasant person.

It was during a visit to the collection of porcelain from Japan in the 17th century at Zwinger Palace that I noticed a vivid red camellia on one of the large 'Imari'[1] vases.

"Do you know if there is a camellia tree in Dresden that came from Japan?"

Martina asked me, looking at the vase.

"No, a real camellia tree? Does such a camellia actually exist?"

"There is a camellia tree in the gardens of a remote palace in the suburbs called Pillnitz that came from Japan 220 years ago."

"Really? I can't believe it."

"It is still very well cared for, and in a few months, it will be in full bloom."

I didn't have time to visit the camellia she was talking about at the time, so I left it at that.

Her words must have remained in my mind for some reason. When I saw the news about the camellia in Japan, I suddenly recalled the conversation about the camellia in Pillnitz.

Yes, I wondered what had happened to that camellia tree. The moment I thought of it, it was the right day. I was no longer bound by the restraints, but I couldn't stay still, so I booked a seat on the plane to Germany. While I was thinking about this, the stewardess, who had been so brusque, spoke to me.

I guessed that she had finished her meal service and had some spare time. Perhaps she felt sorry for me, as I was traveling with a group of mature couples and had no companion.

"Can I get you anything to drink?"

"Do you have any Williams?"

"I'm sorry, we don't have any. I have a cognac."

"Yes, please."

"Coffee or tea, too?"

"Coffee, please. By the way, what's the weather like in Frankfurt?"

"Cloudy, sometimes rainy, four degrees. It's the normal weather for the beginning of March."

She answered with a smile.

The flight was smooth. I read through my research on 'the legend

---

1 Japanese brightly colored porcelains made in northwestern Kyushu.

of the camellia' again, which I had studied before my departure. According to the document, there is indeed a camellia tree in a corner of the Pillnitz court garden. The legend says that a Swedish doctor and botanist named Thunberg brought it back from Japan. He came to Nagasaki, where the Dutch trading factory was located, during the Edo period (1603-1868) and wrote about Japan precisely at that time. But this earnest doctor did not describe the camellia. It was the purpose of my research. I was hoping to get more detailed information on this trip.

The main purpose now was to see the camellia in Dresden, and I had not decided on anything else. It was already late afternoon when I arrived at Frankfurt Airport. I stayed overnight at the hotel I had reserved at the airport.

It is so convenient nowadays that reservations can easily be made on the Internet. There is no need to bother other people at all. Once I have booked my flight, hotel, and car, I can travel around the world with only one small baggage.

Tomorrow, I will have a leisurely breakfast, rent a car from the airport, and head north on the autobahn Route 5, then turn onto Route 4 just before Bad Hersfeld and move on to my destination, Dresden. Since it was winter in Germany and the weather was bad, I had reserved a navigation system for this drive. I would arrive at Dresden by 3:00 p.m. at the latest. First of all, I had to get over my jet lag. With this in mind, I fell into a shallow sleep.

Dresden, the capital of the German state of Saxony, also known as the Baroque capital and the Florence of the North, lies on the banks of the Elbe River. Ten kilometers southeast upwards the Elbe River, a remote palace called Pillnitz retains its elegant appearance at the riverside. After the castle came into the possession of King

August the Strong of Saxony in 1706, he had it reconstructed with the oriental taste prevalent at the time. The roofs are warped in a seemingly Chinese style, creating a somewhat exotic atmosphere. On the western side of the grounds is a large garden where one can take a leisurely stroll.

In one corner there is a glass greenhouse with a curious cylindrical shape. It is 15 meters in diameter and perhaps 13 meters high. Inside there is a large camellia tree. Spring is late here. Even in March, the trees in the garden have not yet awoken from their winter sleep. Inside the greenhouse, however, spring is already in full swing. The large camellia trees are covered with countless red flowers. It even feels as being in a camellia forest. A walkway is leading high up in the greenhouse, where one can walk around the perimeter and look down on the huge camellia trees from above. At the base of the camellia stands a small metal plaque with an explanatory note.

"The camellia was imported from Japan in 1776 and came to Pillnitz as a potted plant via the Kew Botanic Gardens in London. It was planted here already in 1801 by the court gardener Terscheck. A mobile glasshouse was built in 1992 to protect it from the cold, and computer-controlled heating was provided."

I stood looking up at the large camellia tree again and was amazed at its size. And then I was struck by a dim recollection of a bygone era. On the outskirts of Chester, near the west coast of central England, there is a house owned by the Grosvenor family. It must have been 40 years ago now. I once visited the greenhouse with its collection of plants on a day when the gardens were open to the public. I don't remember any more whether there were camellias. I have also seen camellias in orangeries, or greenhouses, as they are called, in castles all over Europe.

How much time had passed? I noticed a young woman standing

next to me.

"Are you surprised?"

She asked me.

I shifted my gaze to the owner of the voice.

She had long black hair, a fair complexion and lips of a fiery crimson. Her pupils were just as black and shiny as her hair.

"Ah, you are from Japan? I was very surprised. It was worth coming all the way from Japan to see this camellia. But is it true that it came here in 1776?"

She smiled at me impressed and said,

"Strictly speaking, the year of the arrival is different. It was very carefully maintained. But, the information in this description is a little wrong."

"What is wrong?"

"The point is that it was sent from the Kew Botanical Gardens in London. That's how it's told to this day, but this camellia came here directly from Japan."

She replied with conviction.

"You know a lot about this camellia, don't you? Are you doing any research here? Actually, I came here to find out more about the legend of this camellia."

I asked again.

"……"

There was a long pause. She did not answer the question, but stared at me with serious, kind, shining eyes.

The expression on her face made me wonder, as if she was asking me a question or commanding me to do something.

"Even so, that it's a huge glass house."

I changed the subject.

In Japan, large-scale greenhouses called tropical botanical gardens have been built in various parts of the country. There are 'traveler's trees' and 'palm trees', which stir up the feeling of travelling to the tropics in visitors' minds. However, it is not every day that a greenhouse is set up for a specific tree.

"This greenhouse is moved over the rails in May and the camellia is left outdoors to leaf out."

There are indeed rails extending into the ground.

"What kind of greenhouse was this in the past?" I asked.

"Of course, they were not used to have such modern greenhouses back then."

"It can get minus 20 degrees in this part of the country in winter."

"In the old days, they used to build a wooden greenhouse in the autumn and build a fire in the furnace next door to bring in the warm air."

"That's a lot of work every year."

"It was the winter of 1905. The heating fire caught fire and burned down the greenhouse."

"Oh, no! What happened to the camellia?"

The fire in the middle of winter made me more and more surprised.

"The fire brigade rushed to the scene and used a water pump to extinguish the fire. The camellia was also engulfed in flames. The firefighters then sprayed water on the camellia, which quickly froze. Though the ice protected the camellia from the fire."

"But the camellia must have been badly damaged?"

"Of course. But in spring, the young shoots sprouted from the burnt branches and came back to life. People were very happy. And it began again, year after year, to produce many beautiful red blossoms."

Surprised by the story of the camellia, I asked further.

"How did this camellia come all the way from Edo period Japan to this land?"

"It was sent by Dr. Thunberg".

"He was a Swedish botanist, I believe?"

"That's right. He came to Dejima[2] in the year of An'ei[3] 5, during the reign of the Tokugawa Shogun I'eharu[4].

"I don't understand why he sent this camellia here and why it was so valued here."

Just as I looked at the woman standing beside me, about to ask for more information, a gust of wind swept through the greenhouse. The branches of the large camellia tree rustled and countless leaves and flowers rustled too. In the midst of this rustle, she murmured, as if ignoring my intentions.

"I must go now."

I could only stare at her beautiful, graceful back as she disappeared into the shade of the camellia tree.

---

[2] An artificial island of Nagasaki Japan. It was served as a trading factory for the Portuguese and the Dutch.

[3] An era name. 1772-1781

[4] The tenth Shogun of Tokugawa Shogunate. (1737-1786)

1. Carl Linnaeus

It was an early summer morning in 1770. Bright sunlight shone through the window of the study, in the house of Professor Carl Linnaeus in Uppsala, about 75 km north of the capital Stockholm. Since his own studies at the Uppsala University and his appointment as a professor here in 1741, his reputation had been growing. Many talented students from all over the world came to the university to follow his classes. These days, his lectures were rarely held at the university; they usually took place in his study at his private house or in the botanical garden which he had built himself on the grounds. Professor Linnaeus, now sixty-three years old, was already an authority on botany, natural history and medicine. At that time, medicine was positioned alongside botany as a field of natural science. Knowledge of medicinal herbs was indispensable for the treatment of diseases, and doctors were expected to acquire expertise in botany.

There was a knock on the door of the study.

"Come in, come in." The man who opened the door and entered was the professor's twenty-seven-year-old student, Carl Peter Thunberg. His name is also known as 'Tsunberi' or 'Tsunberuku' in Japan.

"Mr. Thunberg, thank you for coming so quickly. How are you? Are you making progress with your research?"

"Yes, Professor Linnaeus, I am fine. The research is going well."

"I see. That's good to hear. Well, have a seat. I called you here today because I want to talk to you."

The professor was wearing a long wig, as was the custom in Europe at this time. It was started by the powerful French king, and long hair was the symbol of a strong man. The professor, who had been unwell for some time, stood up slowly, took a thick file from the stack, placed it on his desk and stared at Thunberg's face.

"You know that when I started my natural history studies, I received a scholarship from Uppsala University to explore Lapland in northern Sweden. I wrote a paper on my findings."

"Yes, I have read the paper, Professor Linnaeus."

Thunberg replied, with a look on his face as needless to say. His expression was soft and his confident eyes shone. It was full of tenderness, but at times reminded of the sharpness of a bird of prey. Yet he was never intimidating. In fact, he might have given the impression of a gentle person. The passion within, the power of will to move towards the truth, was concentrated in the sharpness of his gaze.

"Then I went to Holland in 1735, when I was twenty-eight years old, to study medicine there and publish my thesis on the plant taxonomy."

"I have studied your groundbreaking work. What immortalized your name was your clarification of the existence of sexuality in plants, in other words, your elucidation of the mechanisms of stamens and pistils. The other was the establishment of 'the binomial system' for classifying plants and animals."

"That's right. This is a method of describing plants and animals in Latin by genus and species. You know that I named the camellia 'Camellia japonica' (Yabutsubaki), don't you? The camellia was first brought to Europe by Georg Josef Kamel, who was born in Moravia (now the Czech Republic). He had been in the Philippines and probably brought it to Spain around 1700. I named the camellia after him. Camellias are known to grow wild in Japan, that is why I named it Japonica."

"Did you have a plan to go to Japan, too?"

"No, I hadn't thought that far ahead. I had always wanted to go on an expedition to Africa when I was in Holland. But I missed the opportunity and returned to Sweden from Holland because the political situation in Europe was becoming increasingly uncertain. In hindsight, I regret that I had missed this opportunity.

Two years later, in 1740, the war of succession between Prussia and Austria over the succession of the Austrian Habsburgs began. The following year, war broke out between Sweden and Russia. This war, which aimed to regain the territory that our country had lost in 1721, caused tragic devastation in Sweden.

Then, in 1757, another Seven Years' War started between Austria and Prussia. Seeing this as an opportunity, Sweden invaded Prussia and again tried to regain lost ground, but with poor results. In other words, Europe remained in a period of warfare until 1763."

"So, you were active in a time of war."

"Well, then, Mr. Thunberg, now we live in a time of peace. But as I am too old to go to Africa, I'm going to give you that chance. You must make your own future, but before you do, I would like you to develop your knowledge of medicine, would you not?"

Thunberg replied to the professor's unexpected words after a breath. "Yes, sir, thank you. I shall be delighted to accept."

Professor Linnaeus's plump face, which looked much younger than his age, beamed with delight. Looking at the documents on his desk, he continued. It contained the details of Thunberg's research. "Thank you, Mr. Thunberg, I am very pleased to hear your response. You completed your research on 'lymphatic vessels' under me, didn't you? After that, you worked on 'sciatica' under Professor

Sidrén at this university, I believe. As the world progresses, more and more people suffer from back pain. In that sense, your work is really future-oriented."

At that time, it was the custom, unimaginable nowadays, for the professor in charge to write a thesis on the student's research. The professor was satisfied with Thunberg's medical work. But he wanted him to study further and told him,

"Paris would be a good place for you to continue your studies. The scholarship I am applying for you is perfect for your medical studies in France. Furthermore, I am an old friend of Professor Bernard de Jussieu in Paris. He is now at the Botanical Gardens in Paris, and his brothers Antoine and Joseph are also renowned botanists. Their nephew, Antoine Laurent de Jussieu, is about your age. They are the leading family of botanists in France. They will certainly help you with your medical studies."

Thunberg was genuinely touched by the professor's expectation, trust and concern.

"Before you go to Paris, visit my friend in Amsterdam, Holland, the doctor and botanist Professor Burman. Do you know his son, Nicholas Lawrence?"

Thunberg remembered this man well.

"Oh, then. That's convenient."

The professor looked out of the window as if remembering a long time ago.

"When I was in Amsterdam, I lived with the Burmans and they looked after me very well. Later, their son was born, who decided to follow in his father's footsteps and came to me to continue his studies. That was in 1760, I think. When did you enter the university?"

"The following year, 1761, sir. He was a great senior student to me at the time."

Thunberg understood the long-standing and close relationship between his professor and Burman.

"Then you can start by preparing to go to Amsterdam."

"Much appreciated, Professor."

Thunberg left the professor's study with a sense of excitement.

Professor Linnaeus was the leading naturalist of the European world at the time. He sent his students on expeditions and received reports on their information, experiences and knowledge, thus creating a state-of-the-art world information center so to speak. His students were called 'apostles' after those who spread Christianity. Among them was Daniel Solander, whom the professor sent to England to accompany James Cook on his voyage to the South Pacific from 1768. The professor had a high opinion of Thunberg's intelligence and wanted to give him an 'apostolic' mission after his studies in Paris. The destination was Africa, which Thunberg was made clear today.

 Before his departure, there was one more important thing left for Thunberg to do. That was to say goodbye to his girlfriend Birgitta. For some time after Professor Linnaeus had told him that he was going to Paris, he had spent a while wondering how to broach the subject with her.

Birgitta was the daughter of the Ruda family who lodged him during his university days. Her father was his mentor in his studies while Mr. Ruda had Thunberg living in his house.

He had high hopes for his future. It was her father's wish that Birgitta would marry Thunberg when he became an independent doctor in the future. At this time Birgitta was a beautiful eighteen-year-old girl.

Thunberg and Birgitta strolled hand in hand along the paths of the birch forest, where the trees were thick and the summer breeze blew. Birds were singing and the babbling brook made a pleasant sound.

"Birgitta, there's something I need to tell you ..."

He spoke out boldly, but then he hesitated.

"What's wrong? It's not like you."

Birgitta gave him a quizzical look.

He stopped, grabbed Birgitta's hands firmly and looked into her blue eyes. A soft breeze gently brushed her blonde curls.

"Actually, I'm going to Paris ..."

"Carl, you are finally going abroad. I know that a lot of people who study with Professor Linnaeus go abroad. But I'm relieved to hear you are going to Paris. In this case it is not such a long period of time that you will be there, is it?"

Birgitta had a vague sense that this day would come. But when she heard where he was going, she felt proud of him in spite of the fact that he would leave her soon.

A brilliant young man like him will go abroad to continue his studies and eventually comes back to her with honors.

"Of course. I don't think my studies at the University of Paris will last that long."

Thunberg replied in a cheerful voice.

Birgitta buried her face in his chest. The parting tears wetting her cheeks melted the words she tried to utter into them. They exchanged a sad but cheerful kiss.

When Thunberg left Uppsala on 13 August, 1770, he was carrying a letter of recommendation from Professor Linnaeus to the governor-general in Cape Governorate and a small diary. It was containing the names of the people he had met during his nearly nine-year journey halfway around the world. On 9 August, before his departure, Professor Linnaeus wrote a parting word in this diary. It was a proverb from the Roman poet Vergil. *To make a name for oneself by one's achievements is the work of virtue.*

Professor Linnaeus's expectations for him were high.

2. Johannes Burman

After leaving Uppsala, Thunberg returned to Jönköping, his home town, 300 km south-west of the university city, to say goodbye to his family. He was born in this town on the shores of Lake Vättern. When he was seven years old, his father died. His father ran a small business and aside from that he worked for a limestone production company on the other side of the river, as well as accountant as for recording the limestone scales.

However, he was not rich enough to leave a fortune to his surviving wife and two sons. His wife, Margareta, worked hard and managed to pay for the children's education out of the family's meagre finances. Eventually, Thunberg's mother remarried. When he finished primary school, his new father and mother wanted him to pursue a career as a tradesman. However, Thunberg's primary school teacher had recognized his intelligence and was keen to encourage his parents to send him on an academic path. Thus, in 1761, at the age of 18, Thunberg entered the Uppsala University, where he pursued his studies until this day nine years later.

Thunberg said goodbye to his old friends back home and set off for Helsingborg on the west coast. There he boarded a boat and arrived in Helsingør, Denmark, on the other side of the channel, only four kilometers apart. On the shore rises Kronborg Castle, the setting of Shakespeare's Hamlet. From there he went south to the capital, Copenhagen where he met a friend from the Uppsala University. During a tour of the botanical gardens, they had the opportunity to discuss their dreams for the future.

From Copenhagen, he sailed around Skagen at the tip of the Jutland peninsula, out into the North Sea and saw the Dutch island of Texel. The island of Texel is one of the archipelagos of West Friesian Islands, and the winds blowing in from the North Sea have formed sand dunes on the island, a landscape unfamiliar to him. Finally, he reached Amsterdam. A large number of cargoes were being unloaded from ships that had just arrived from distant Batavia (present-day Jakarta, Indonesia) via the African Cape Governorate (present-day Cape Town). He was struck by the exotic sight of Batavians and black South Africans.

When he disembarked, it was already dusk in early winter. The houses facing the canals were beginning to be lit. He quickly landed and unpacked his travelling luggage at a nearby inn. From his window, he saw busy streets with people coming and going. For a few days he spent time exploring the city of Amsterdam. Professor Linnaeus had informed of his visit in a letter to Burman.

On the morning of his planned visit, he got into a carriage from his inn and set off for the University of Amsterdam. He arrived at his destination shortly after crossing several canals. Professor Johannes Burman, whom he was visiting, taught at the university, which was founded in 1632. Compared to Uppsala University, it was a smaller building, but it had a historical character. When he asked for directions at the porter's lodge, a tall, elderly gatekeeper with a good-natured look smiled at Thunberg and led him inside. A tall, old man with a grey-haired wig, the same age as Professor Linnaeus, greeted him.

In contrast to Linnaeus, who had a very scholarly air, Burman, although a scholar, was also an executive of the Dutch East India Company and had the gravitas of a practitioner befitting a leading economic figure.

"Is that you, Mr. Thunberg? I received a letter from Professor Linnaeus and have been waiting for you."

Burman talked kindly to him in Latin. The scholars had no difficulty in communicating with each other, as they had used Latin at university.

"How was the ship trip?"

"The North Sea waves were calm and the journey via Denmark was pleasant."

"How is Professor Linnaeus?"

"He is very well, but recently he has some minor problems with his health."

Thunberg gave a detailed account of the professor's recent condition.

"Well, that's worrying. I hope he will remain in good health for a long time."

Thunberg could feel his old friend's concern for his wellbeing.

"I hear you are going to Paris to study medicine."

"Yes, I have already completed my studies at Uppsala University and intend to further deepen my medical knowledge in Paris."

Thunberg said in a confident voice.

"Very good. That's why Professor Linnaeus recommended you. You can stay at my house until you leave for Paris. Professor Linnaeus lived in my house for a time when he was young. I have also invited my son Nicholas for dinner. Let's take our time and listen to what you have to say. I have to leave now for a meeting, but someone here will bring you back to my house."

Thunberg was moved and grateful, and saw the professor off as he left the room.

Thunberg got off from his guide's carriage and arrived at the Burman's house. The professor's house also faced a canal and was a magnificent mansion with a narrow facade but with a great depth. The interior was also luxurious. A young servant girl showed him to a room upstairs, reserved for guests. It was a beautifully decorated drawing room. Detailed still-life paintings of flowers and fish hung on the walls. On the mantelpiece was a beautiful porcelain vase.

"I hope you will be able to relax until dinner. If you need anything else, please call on me."

With these words, the servant left.

Thunberg unpacked his luggage and freshened up. He opened the window to watch the boats passing by on the canal which led to the port of Amsterdam, and from there to the North Sea, past the Strait of Dover, reaching the Atlantic Ocean, and .... Thunberg never tired of staring at the canal, imagining the new days ahead.

Towards the evening the same servant girl knocked at the door.

"Lady and gentlemen, they are all here."

He was led downstairs to the dining room, where three members of the Burman family were waiting for him. The professor introduced his wife, Adriane.

"You are Mr. Thunberg? I have heard about you from my son. I also know you from Professor Linnaeus's letters. Please make yourself feel at home."

He shook hands with the elegant Mrs. Burman and looked at Nicholas, who was standing next to her.

With a youthful laugh the young man held his old friend's hand tightly and said:

"Hey, it's really been a long time since we last met. I'm glad to see you are well. I hear you're finally going on an adventure. I wonder how Professor Linnaeus is doing."

The conversation was full of mutual updates on each other's recent activities.

Soon a lively meal began. The professor raised his glass and toasted Thunberg's visit and his studies in Paris.

Fish that had been landed in Amsterdam's harbor and freshly prepared was brought to the table. It was a large sole accompanied by rare sliced lemons.

"These lemons are from my greenhouse." Burman said proudly.

Thunberg recalled that his professor Linnaeus also had a greenhouse in his garden where he grew tropical plants.

In between meals, Thunberg's gaze fell on the cupboards in the dining room. There were a number of colorful porcelain pieces on display.

"That's Japanese porcelain called Arita-yaki[5]," he said.

The professor further pointed to a jar on the small desk in the living room. It had a red flower on it.

"That also came from Japan. They are very rare these days. By the way, are you interested in porcelain?"

Thunberg shook his head from side to side, surprised by the question outside his area of expertise.

"It's a bit long, but I'll tell you about porcelain."

Thunberg put his cutlery on the table and listens to the story of porcelain for the first time. "When it comes to porcelain, we must start with Augustus the Strong, King of Saxony in Germany."

Burman's tone sounded like a university lecture.

"Frederick August I, born in 1670, was a colorful figure known in Europe as King of Saxony. You will know that after 1697 he combined the titles of King of Poland and Grand Duke of Lithuania and became August II. His interest in architecture was great, and he built the splendid Baroque Zwinger Palace in Dresden. The Chinese-style villa in the suburb of Pillnitz also belonged to him."

Here the professor took a break and sipped the newly poured white wine.

"This is where the Dutch East India Company played a major role. The King's interest in porcelain was deep and the collection he purchased from this company was vast. Large quantities of porcelain were brought to Europe from Japan, including products of the Qing dynasty after the fall of the Ming dynasty. The profits of the East India Company, which monopolized trade with Japan, were enormous at the time.

In order to maintain close relations with Saxony, the Dutch Minister purchased a large mansion opposite the Zwinger Palace across the Elbe. The building was called the 'Dutch Palace'. King August the Strong later acquired this building and wanted to use it to display his collection of porcelain.

This plan was not realized, but many of his collections were displayed at the celebrations held there. The building was subsequently rebuilt several times, with the roof having an oriental, warped shape. Since then, the building has been known as the 'Japanese Palace' and has survived to this day."

Thunberg admired the passion of the powerful sovereign.

The professor continued.

"Here appears an alchemist, Johann Friedrich Böttger, born in 1682. He began his training as a pharmacist in Berlin, Prussia, but developed an interest in alchemy, the art of turning cheap metal into gold. In front of skeptical people about alchemy he turned silver coins into gold. Whatever the trick was that he used, word gradually spread.

---

5   A broad term of Japanese porcelain made in the area around the town of Arita, northwestern Kyushu Island.

This finally came to the attention of King Frederick I of Prussia. The king expressed his willingness to employ him, but Böttger fled, believing that his imposture would be exposed and his safety endangered. The angry king put a bounty on his head to track him down. He narrowly escaped with his life and finally fled to his uncle in neighboring Saxony, where the bounty was ineffective.

The incident caused a stir and eventually reached the ears of King August the Strong. The Strong King took a great interest in the alchemist. This eventually led to a dispute with Frederick I over Böttger, i.e., a conflict between countries. In the end, King August the Strong won the dispute and Böttger was brought to Dresden and forced to experiment with alchemy."

Thunberg was surprised at the unexpected turn of events in the professor's story.

"In the basement of the palace, an alchemy laboratory was set up, equipped exactly as Böttger wanted. Two more chemists joined him. They were von Tschirnhaus and von Ohain. Apart from alchemy, August the Strong had also ordered von Tschirnhaus to make a prototype of the porcelain imported from Japan and Qing, in order to see if he could somehow produce it himself.

Von Tschirnhaus knew that alchemy was a fraud and told Böttger that it would be better for him to study porcelain. It was only a secret to King August the Strong. Böttger agreed and changed his research to the development of porcelain.

In 1705, fears of war spread and the laboratory was moved from the palace cellars in Dresden to Meissen on the lower Elbe River. There the three men moved to a laboratory in the Albrechtsburg castle and spurred the development of porcelain. However, with the outbreak of war with Sweden, it was no longer safe there either. So Böttger was moved to the impregnable fortress of Königstein in southern Saxony. They continued their research there for a year, but the experimental facilities were inadequate, so they moved to a fortress in Dresden called Jungfernbastei, where they finally succeeded in producing porcelain in 1706. This was brown porcelain, later known as Böttger porcelain. Satisfied with the production of porcelain, which was not the original purpose of making gold, August the Strong set up a full-scale production factory in Meissen. As head of Meissen, Böttger finally succeeded in producing white porcelain in 1707. It was the beginning of Meissen porcelain, which continues to this day. This meant that August the Strong no longer needed to buy porcelain from the East India Company and decided to develop it into a major industry that would enrich the Saxon treasury.

A decree of 1710 established the 'Royal Electorate of Saxony Porcelain Production Company'. In 1714, Böttger was finally released from his long imprisonment. However, he was still forced to live a life of captivity in Saxony in order to keep the production of Meissen porcelain secret. However, he was unable to give up on his youthful dream of alchemy. He was finally allowed to continue his research, but in 1719 at the age of 37, he died from toxic gases inhaled during an experiment. His alchemy was never perfected, but he was able to create a groundbreaking invention: porcelain."

"It's a bizarre story, isn't it?"

said Thunberg, who had been listening to Professor Burman with admiration.

"It goes back a little further than that, but after the fall of the Ming and the rise of the Qing in China, foreign trade was banned in 1656. Japanese porcelain was exported to Europe to fill the gap. It was the foresight of the East India Company, which was based in Japan."

The professor's gaze turned to the 'Arita'-porcelain jar on the small desk.

"It was made by a master potter called Kakiemon, and was particularly beautiful with its red flowers on a white background."

Thunberg also gazed at the jar and asked,

"Those flowers are camellias, aren't they?"

The professor smiled at Thunberg's words.

"Indeed. Have you ever seen a real camellia?"

Nicholas, who had not joined the professor's conversation until now, opened his mouth with a laugh.

"Ha-ha-ha," said Nicholas,

"Father, don't you know there are two camellia bushes in the botanical garden in Uppsala?"

Nicholas and Thunberg looked at each other and laughed. Apparently, the two young men knew more about camellias than the professor.

This time Thunberg explained to the professor.

"A man called Lagerström, who has the title of commercial adviser, brought two plants of tea (Camellia sinensis) from China. As we know, the custom of drinking tea has recently become widespread in Sweden and interest in tea cultivation has increased. Professor Linnaeus and other plant experts were of the opinion that the leaves of the tea were not quite right and that they were a little too big. Eventually, the tea shrubs blossomed. It turned out to be a camellia. In China tea as a plant was forbidden for export at that time, so the merchant was cheated."

Then a dessert and tea were brought to the table.

"This is a tea called 'Keemun', brought from China, and it has a very beautiful color."

The professor took a sip and continued.

"Just as the production of porcelain began in Europe, a new policy was implemented in Japan. In 1715, a brilliant academic politician named 'Hakuseki Arai' advised the Tokugawa Shogun to restrict the total volume of trade."

The professor's knowledge was rich and his talk inexhaustible.

"What exactly do you mean by total volume of trade?" Thunberg asked.

"To summarize briefly, it means this. The Tokugawa Shogunate, which had already implemented a policy of isolation, limiting foreign trade to Nagasaki, tightened its restrictions even further. In other words, in order to prevent the loss of gold and silver to the rest of the world, they reduced the volume of trade in order to stop the worsening of the Shogunate's financial situation. The order was to reduce the number of ships coming from the Qing to 30 per year, with a trade value of 6,000 kan (approx. 22,400 kg) of silver, and to only two ships from the Netherlands, with a trade value of 3,000 kan (approx. 11,200 kg) of silver."

When the professor confirmed that everyone understood, he continued.

"This meant that bulky cargoes such as porcelain could no longer be traded."

The professor continued his explanation with simple words so that Thunberg could understand.

"This is why the price of Japanese porcelain suddenly skyrocketed."

Thunberg looked at the jar on the small desk and wondered how much the 'Arita'-porcelain on display was worth.

"Most likely in Qing, foreign trade had resumed and cheap porcelain was being imported.

However, there were those who insisted that the porcelain had to be made in Japan."

"But wasn't Europe's own professional porcelain production in Meissen already started?"
Thunberg asked.

"That's right. Since 1710, the production of porcelain in Saxony had been carried out under strict secrecy in order to protect the know-how. The process was divided up into small steps, so that the whole picture could not be grasped. However, each country sent industrial spies to Meissen in order to discover the secrets of porcelain production. One of them, the porcelain production chemist Samuel Stolzel, finally escaped to Austria with the secret. Under the patronage of King Charles VI of the Holy Roman Empire, he was able to build a porcelain manufacturing factory in its capital, Vienna, at the end of 1718. This was Meissen's first competitor, the 'Augarten'.

The Dupois brothers, who had also worked at Meissen, went to Paris and opened the 'Sèvres' factory in 1738. Once technology has been leaked, it is not easy to keep it secret.

In 1747, the 'Fürstenberg' was produced in Hanover. In England, Wedgwood, although not porcelain, was opened in 1759. Whether Japan's economic policy was effective or not, I do not know. It is a fact that those trade restrictions accelerated the development of porcelain in Europe."

Then his son Nicholas said:

"When a country uses its power to restrict or ban an export item, that's what drives the development of alternatives."

The professor added an explanation of recent trends in Meissen porcelain.

"In the beginning," he said, "many of the pieces had an East Asian look, imitating motifs from China or Japan. But gradually, they were decorated with unique European patterns. To a painter who had never seen a pomegranate this exotic fruit must have looked like an onion. The onion pattern is unique to Meissen and was actively produced since 1740. A particular European development was the addition of sculptural elements to porcelain. Already from the time of August the Strong, animal forms and dolls began to be manufactured in addition to plates and bowls for court use. Masters such as Kirchner and Kendler made large sculptural porcelain. Nowadays, the shape of the figures has become smaller and the main trend changed to miniaturized dolls and animal miniatures which became more dominant. Apart from this classical trend, Sèvres and Wedgwood also developed their own styles. Thus, the European ceramics industry is now in a period of design competition."

That night Thunberg suddenly felt like an expert on porcelain.

The next day, the Burmans showed Thunberg the valuable natural history specimens from all over the world that they had collected at their home. His garden, an 'English-style garden' had been created, with plants that Thunberg had never seen before. Burman also gave him free use of his library, which contained his own extensive collection of books. At that time the University of Amsterdam was small and professors often lectured at home.

He also introduced him to Professor van Rooyen from the Leiden University. The botanical garden of the university contained many exotic plants brought by the East India Company and Thunberg was able to closely observe all these interesting plants.

His son Nicholas kept many specimens of Swedish minerals, plants and seaweeds that he had collected while studying at the Uppsala University. However, they did not have names. Nicholas asked Thunberg to identify and to add the taxonomy. He completed the task without any difficulty. Thunberg had submitted his doctoral thesis for medicine before leaving Uppsala and had a clear memory of what the specimens were. He did not need to use any reference books.

When Burman found out about it from his son, he was amazed by Thunberg's knowledge and began to think about refining it.

"Yes, let's send him to Batavia on an East India Company ship as a naturalist!"

Burman immediately asked Thunberg's idea about his intention.

"I too am very interested in Batavia. I will gladly accept your offer." Thunberg replied with burning enthusiasm.

But despite his words, he thought about his girlfriend Birgitta. He remembered his promise to her that he would return as soon as he had finished his studies in Paris. What to tell her....

Thunberg spent his days in Amsterdam, which he found enjoyable and meaningful, but something stuck in his mind.

It was at the beginning of December, when the last leaves had fallen from the trees and it started feeling cold, that he left the Burmans and set off for Paris. From Amsterdam, he took a ship through the Strait of Dover, via Le Havre in France, along the Seine to the town of Rouen, with its towering Gothic cathedral, Thunberg was overwhelmed by its majesty. From here, he travelled overland to Paris instead of by boat. It was dark after the short winter sun had set when he passed through the walls of Paris. He got out of the carriage and found a hostel nearby, where he spent his first night in Paris.

Amsterdam was a big city, but this city was huge. Even at night, the hustle and bustle outside was still going on. People were enjoying the nightlife in a way that the countryside-bred Thunberg could never have imagined. The women seduced men in the street with their flirtatious behavior. In the playhouses, unimaginable beauties put on a glamorous performance. Dressed divas sang joyful songs with voices like birds and suddenly the melody turned pathetic and earnestly appealed to the audience. Thunberg lost track of time.

After spending a few days in Paris, Thunberg finally set off for the Paris Botanical Gardens. After a short drive from the inn, the carriage crossed the Pont Neuf over the Seine. Following the river up the Seine, on his left he saw the magnificent Notre-Dame on the Île de la Cité. Thunberg was again awed by its Gothic cathedral. Soon he could see the island of Saint-Louis. The carriage continued at a light pace until they arrived at their destination, the Botanical Gardens.

"I would like to talk to Professor Bernard de Jussieu please."

Thunberg announced his visit at the entrance. The gatekeeper was kind enough to take his travel bag and led him inside. He was shown into a room on the first floor of a large building. After waiting a short while, Bernard de Jussieu, a well-dressed man with an eagle nose, entered the room. He was born in 1699 and was eight years older than Professor Linnaeus.

"Welcome. You must be Mr. Thunberg. I've been expecting you. I received a letter from Professor Linnaeus."

Thunberg greeted him politely and handed him a letter of recommendation from his former professor.

"How is Professor Linnaeus? I heard that he had some health issues. …… And your purpose for studying abroad was to study medicine, wasn't it?"

To the professor, Thunberg explained in detail his study intensions abroad.

"I see. You are going on board an East India Company ship. My younger brother Joseph is also a botanist and is currently in South America. It seems life there is not so easy."

The professor's family were prestigious French botanists. His elder brother Antoine, also a renowned botanist, was the director of the

Royal Botanical Garden in Paris.

"By the way, my nephew is here too." he said. "Let me introduce him to you."

With these words, the professor rang the bell which was on his desk. He told the man who entered, to call his nephew. A few moments later, a young man arrived.

"This is my nephew, Antoine Laurent, who has recently graduated from the university and has been offered a position here at the Botanical Garden."

The young man beamingly exchanged a firm handshake with Thunberg. He would later go on to develop the Linnaean taxonomy and become director of the National Museum of Natural History, which was set up after the French Revolution to separate from the Botanical Garden.

Antoine Laurent spoke to Thunberg.

"Are you about to embark on an adventure tour of the world?"

Thunberg told him why he had come to Paris.

"It is not clear yet where I should go. But, possibly from Cape Governorate to Batavia. For this purpose, I will now expand my studies of medicine in Paris."

Then Professor de Jussieu said to his nephew.

"You are just out of the university, so you must be familiar with the inner workings. You will be able to show Mr. Thunberg around at the university and take him to the university dormitory, where he's settling in."

"With pleasure. Before that, I'll show you the Royal Botanical Garden. There are many unusual things here."

The young man's story was fascinating. His three uncles were all botanists, and from an early age he had been surrounded by exotic plants from all over the world. So, he was already developing the ambition to be considered the new head of the French Botanical Academy.

Antoine Laurent gave a tour of the Botanical Garden and explained its history.

The history of this Botanical Garden can be traced back to the Royal Herbarium founded by Louis XIII in 1633. The purpose of its establishment was to counter the authority of the Sorbonne at that time. In 1635, it was opened to the public. This is not just a botanical garden. It is a place where botany, chemistry, animal anatomy and other subjects are lectured by outstanding scholars.

Surprised by the mild Parisian climate, which was far milder than the Uppsala winters, Thunberg thus took his first steps in his studies. He studied anatomy, surgery and obstetrics at the University of Paris, at the Hôtel Dieu and Hôspital de la Charité. The Hôtel Dieu in particular had a long history as hospital, dating back to 661 AD. It was a great surprise to find that it operated under the then progressive philosophy of keeping patients in hospital until they had fully recovered. Thunberg's stay in Paris lasted only eight months, but it was very significant that he came into contact with French cutting-edge medicine.

There is one more thing that must be mentioned during his stay in Paris. In February 1771, His Royal Highness Prince Gustav, then Crown Prince, visited Paris and met Thunberg and several other Swedish citizens.

Thunberg also spoke enthusiastically to this nobleman about his future plans.

Two days later, His Highness received the news of his father's sudden death and succeeded to the Swedish throne as King Gustav III. The following year he took the power into his own hands and brought an era of prosperity to the country. This period of prosperity, known as the 'Age of Freedom', lasted until the king's death in 1792. It was in Paris that Thunberg spent the dawn of this new era, so to speak.

In his absence, Burman worked hard to give concrete form to his ideas. In the meantime, it became clear that Japan, and not Batavia, should be Thunberg's final destination. The main reason for this was the lack of information on the Japanese botanical world in Europe, and the request to bring rare Japanese plants. Sending a disciple of Linnaeus was a good way to achieve this.

Until then, it had been known that the climate in Japan was similar to that of The Netherlands. If Japanese plants could be imported, they could be multiplied and sold to other countries, thereby recouping the investment. Fortunately, the East India Company had a monopoly trading base at Dejima in Nagasaki. At the time, sending naturalists on expeditionary voyages was not only fraught with great risk, but also required a large amount of investment capital. To raise the money, Burman approached a number of influential people for investment. Eventually, the mayor of Amsterdam, an executive of the East India Company and a wealthy men agreed to invest.

Burman then wrote to Linnaeus, explaining what had happened and requesting permission to send Thunberg to Japan.

Linnaeus received Burman's letter, but he had recently been feeling depressed by the series of accidents involving the loss of his 'apostles'. Encouraged by Burman's enthusiastic letter, however, he wrote a favorable reply with his consent for sending Thunberg to Japan.

Meanwhile, in Paris, Thunberg wrote to Linnaeus about Burman's proposal. He was well aware that his professor's assistance was essential for such a grand plan.

"While I was in Holland last year, Professor Burman proposed that

I go to Batavia as a naturalist. But I told him that I had never done such a great voyage before and that I did not have the financial means to make it possible. He promised to try to make it happen. Then a few days ago I received a letter from him. In it, he told me that he had finally decided on Japan as my destination. My departure will be in the autumn of this year."

Linnaeus's answer to Thunberg's letter was,

"The voyage to Japan will be full of dangers. But the experience and results of the years there will be ten times greater than those we can achieve in our own country. Reports from botanical specialists and on Japan are few and very limited. But imagine, you are about to become the third scientist to have spent time in Japan, after Cleyer and Kaempfer. That promises a bright future for you. To get to Japan, you have to go via the Cape of Good Hope. It's a chance to kill two birds with one stone. And you could also do some research in Africa."

Thunberg also wrote to Birgitta explaining the situation.

"My dear Birgitta,

I hope you are well; I'm doing very well too and spending my days in Paris in good spirits. The research here is very advanced and interesting. It is stimulating and fascinating in a way that I could never have imagined in Uppsala, and it adds brilliance and depth to my knowledge.

However, I am writing this letter today because I have something to tell you. The fact is that once I have finished my studies in Paris, I will return to Amsterdam and take my medical examination there. That is also a prerequisite for going to distant Japan. Unfortunately, the promise I made to you — that I would return to my hometown after my studies in Paris — is not going to happen any time soon. You must be saddened. I am also sad that I will be further and further away from you. But I feel as if there is some great force pushing me. I will write to you again when I return to Amsterdam, remembering the kisses on the paths of the forest during the summer in my hometown.

From your Carl."

In July 1771, he returned to Amsterdam and once again became a guest of the Burmans.

During his second stay in Amsterdam, Thunberg successfully passed his exams to become a surgeon and was finally hired as an employee of the East India Company. In December of that year, he was to leave Amsterdam for the Cape Governorate in South Africa as a doctor for the East India Company. His official status at that time was 'part-time surgeon'. The reason for this was, that, unlike full-time doctors, he did not have to be on board the ship at all times. He had the advantage of being able to concentrate on his research at the Cape for an arbitrary period of time.

Before his departure, the Burmans gave a banquet to celebrate Thunberg's grand journey. Many influential people from the city, Leiden University, the University of Amsterdam and the East India Company were invited. Burman, as host, greeted the guests.

"Ladies and Gentlemen. Here is a young man from Sweden, Mr. Thunberg, who is about to leave for Batavia via the Cape Governorate as a member of the East India Company. He is also about to travel from there to faraway Japan. Trade with Japan has not been very profitable in recent decades.

However, in terms of academic research, interesting areas remain unknown. I urge you, Mr. Thunberg, to collect and send a number of valuable plants to the Botanical Gardens. I would like to mention that he has been funded by all you here for this purpose. We wish him a good journey and great success."

Thunberg was happy when seeing the good intentions of so many people.

But when he thinks of Birgitta, his happiness is overshadowed by a dark shade.

He wrote to Birgitta.

"My darling Birgitta,

I am unable to come to see you now, even though you are across the sea. And I am sailing further afield. I can't even imagine what my future will look like. All I can tell you now is that I will come back to you. Even in the unknown, my heart is always with you. My heart belongs to you, my beloved.

I give you a kiss from my heart.

Your Carl"

A few days before Thunberg left Amsterdam, he received a letter and a parcel from his professor Linnaeus. The letter read:

"Mr. Thunberg, I hope your training in France has been worthwhile. I have decided to present you with a book that I would like to give you before you finally leave for Japan. I have already mentioned Doctor Kaempfer. He went to Japan on a long adventure and had a valuable experience. He wrote a very interesting book about his adventurous travels, which has been widely read by posterity: 'the History of Japan', published in England after his death. Take this book with you. It will be an important guide for you during your stay in Japan."

The professor's letter concluded with the following words.

"In 1683 Kaempfer also left Uppsala."

3. Engelbert Kaempfer

They have another heavy squall today. Tropical rain is unusual. It is as if there is a big river in the sky from which the water pours down. While listening to the heavy rain, Kaempfer had a job interview with Dr. Andreas Cleyer, an executive of the East India Company.
"The Governorate of Batavia was established in 1619. At that time the town was called Jayakarta, but the Dutchman Jan Pieterszoon Coen, the future governor-general, occupied it after a struggle with the British. So, it was named Batavia after the Latin name of The Netherlands."
Cleyer was giving Kaempfer an overview of the history of the Governorate of Batavia. He was a large man of stout build. His square face was confident and dignified, and to Kaempfer it seemed as if he was witnessing the authority of the East India Company. Eventually he looked at Kaempfer's curriculum vitae and switched their conversation from Dutch to German.
"Full name is Engelbert Kaempfer. Born 1651 in Lemgo, Westphalia, Germany. What a coincidence!"
Cleyer looked at Kaempfer's face staringly again.
 Kaempfer's life path to date has been quite tumultuous, even for his time. His appearance gave little indication of his mental toughness that had traversed the stormy seas. His face was soft, but his eyes were full of intelligence. His dark, thick eyebrows clearly showed the strength of his will.
"After such a long time I can talk again to a fellow countryman in the language of my country. I was born in Kassel."

For Kaempfer, who had just arrived in Batavia, the East India Company's Asian headquarters, the surprises were not all rain like Noah's flood. He was told that the executive he was interviewing was from the same country.

"Dr. Cleyer, is it true? It's only a day's journey by horse."

"Life is strange. It's a real luck, meeting a man from back home here in Batavia, near the equator. Now, Mr. Kaempfer, why don't you tell me how you got here?"

"Yes, I will. It's a long story, if you don't mind."

"Mr. Kaempfer, time stands still here. The seasons don't change, it's just the monotony of the sun rising and setting. The story of how you got here must be a tumultuous one. I would love to hear it."

"Let me begin with my background. I was born the second son of a pastor and left home at an early age to study history and languages at the Latin school in Hameln and later in Lüneburg and Lübeck."

"These are all venerable cities in the north of Germany. To study at schools in different parts of the country from an early age is a sign of your excellence."

"Then I studied philosophy, history and medicine in Danzig, Torun, Krakow and Königsberg. At the age of 30, I became a member of the academy at Uppsala University in Sweden."

When Cleyer heard of Kaempfer's educational background, he recognized him as a rare talent.

"You've moved around a lot since you were young," he said. "I would think that there would be more to it than just your talents."

"That's right. My two uncles were executed as a result of the witch trials. I wanted to get as far away as possible from my home town, where such barbaric customs persist."

Witch trials, also known as witch hunts, sometimes victimized men as well as women.

"Indeed, our country has been ravaged by a long war and still retains the darkness of the old world. I was born in 1634, during the so-called Thirty Years' War."

Having said this, Cleyer spoke with a somber face about the disastrous wars of German history.

"In the first place, this war began in Bohemia in 1618, long before I was born. In the beginning, it was a religious war between the new and the old Christianity. However, in 1625, Christian IV, King of Denmark, entered the war on the side of the new religion, and England, The Netherlands, Sweden and France joined him, leading to a world war against the Habsburgs, the allies of the Holy Roman Empire.

In 1631, Gustav II of Sweden invaded Germany. Germany was overrun and deepened its desolation. However, Gustav II was killed the following year near Leipzig. Sweden, having lost control of the war, allowed France to intervene, and by the time I was born, from 1635 to 1648, fighting had become relatively calm but was still intermittent. Finally, in 1648, people realized the folly of fighting over religion, and the Treaty of Westphalia was signed, ending the long war."

Outside, the heavy rain had stopped before long and the tropical sunshine had returned. A Batavian servant entered the room with a basket of fruit and crockery.

"Just as well," he said. "Let's have a short break."

Cleyer then offered Kaempfer fresh palm juice and a papaya.

After they had enjoyed the tropical delicacies, the long conversation continued.

"I digress. So, you went to Uppsala University, right?"

"Yes, I did. That's where I met the German naturalist Dr. Samuel von Pufendorf. He was the man who introduced me to King

Charles XI of Sweden."

After the bloody battles with the Holy Roman Empire in the Thirty Years' War, Sweden was no longer cautious about engaging directly with continental Europe. However, The Netherlands, Britain, France, Spain and Portugal were expanding into the Atlantic and other parts of the Indian Ocean. They realized that they had been completely left out of the new world trend while they were preoccupied with a long and futile war.

Is there any way to get out into the world? The king was advised to form an alliance with Persia. An overland route to Asia via Russia was proposed, and a delegation was organized to be sent to Persia via Russia.

"Being part of it I was to accompany them as doctor and secretary. The head of the mission was a Dutchman, Ludwig Fabrizius. In March 1683, two years after arriving in Uppsala, the mission left Stockholm, Sweden."

"Oh, you mean that they followed the land instead of the sea to go to a foreign country? It's surprising, I thought the Swedes were descended from the Vikings and were a maritime nation."

"After passing through Finland, the mission arrived in Moscow. Russia was in a period of political unrest after the death of Tsar Mikhailovich. But they were able to have an audience with Peter, a member of the imperial family who was only ten years old."

This Peter was the man who later ascended to the throne of Russia and led Russia to great power, leaving his name in history as Peter the Great. When he came of age and assumed political power, he sent missions to the leading European countries of the time, and even accompanied them as a member of their delegations himself. In Amsterdam, he worked as a ship's carpenter in the shipyards of the East India Company, according to an anecdote.

"In November the Swedish mission then arrived by land at Astrakhan on the northern shore of the Caspian Sea. They crossed the Caspian Sea by boat and spent a month in the Persian territory of Silwan (now Azerbaijan) surveying oil. Here are some sketches from that time."

Kaempfer then took a drawing book from his bag and showed it to Cleyer.

"You're quite good at drawing, I can understand the world better than I can imagine it here. It's like a world where the air is dry and there is no water."

"That's right. The report on the oil fields in Baku was submitted to the head of the mission. It's probably the first time Europe has heard about it."

"I'm sure it is. I hope he will make use of it."

"In January of the following year, the delegation passed through northern Safavid Persia, Rasht on the southern coast of the Caspian Sea and reached its final destination, the capital Isfahan, in March, one year after leaving Stockholm."

"I see. So, it took them a whole year to reach their destination."

"The mission's goal of establishing an alliance with Persia, however, failed to attract the interest of the Persian king, who already had trade with The Netherlands. The mission had no choice but to return home. But I could not bring myself to go home."

"I see. I see. You have come all the way to Persia. I know exactly how you feel."

"During my stay in Isfahan, I heard that a fleet of Dutch ships was anchored in the southern port town of Bandar Abbas. My heart was violently shaken. I am not sure I would have been able to get on board. I could reach faraway Batavia on an East India Company ship, I thought. I had second thoughts, but I made up my mind to

leave the mission and told Commander Fabrizius of my intention."
"What was his answer?"
"He replied well and readily agreed. Perhaps the Commander had some regret about having to return home without having achieved his goal. He introduced me to Dr. de Jager, a Dutchman who had come to Isfahan."
Kaempfer's face showed joy.
"I immediately went to see Dr. Herbert de Jager. He was an orientalist and an employee of the East India Company. Thankfully he was accommodating and helpful. But he couldn't just decide on his own. We had to get the approval of the head office in Amsterdam."
"Certainly, he would not have had the authority in terms of personnel. In Batavia, he would have had the same decision-making power as in the Amsterdam headquarters."
As an executive of the East India Company, he was well aware of the situation.
"It was in December 1684 that I received the long-awaited letter from the Dutch headquarter. I was hired as an employee of the East India Company, as I had hoped, and was assigned to work in the port city of Bandar Abbas. I immediately packed my bags and left Isfahan. The journey for the assignment was quite interesting. In Persepolis, I was able to investigate Roman ruins and study the ancient Persian 'cuneiform script'. Once I arrived at Bandar Abbas I concentrated on my work."
"It must have been quite busy there, with ships from India stopping over."
"Eventually, however, my health suffered greatly in this place and I was advised to rest and recuperate in the northern part of the country where the climate was better. There I discovered date palms and, while resting, wrote a paper on 'date palms'."

"Turn anything to profit, isn't it?"
"I went back to Bandar Abbas again and continued working there. But when I saw the ships coming into the harbor, I had a sudden urge to board one. When I asked my boss for a transfer to Batavia, he readily accepted. He had always heard that there was a shortage of people there. It was June 1688 when I boarded the East India Company's sailing ship 'Copelle' as ship's doctor. It had been more than five years since I left Stockholm. Mid-July, I arrived in Muscat, the capital of Oman. I stayed there for only a few days, but I was able to make many sketches and record many things."
Kaempfer showed Cleyer the sketches he made there.
"Then I continued my journey by ship and arrived in India in August. After a month's stay, I went to Ceylon (now Sri Lanka), where I stayed until May 1689. That island is in the tropics, but there are high mountains and different climatic zones. It was an interesting place and I stayed there for a long time. In the tropics, the diseases are very different. I immediately started researching tropical diseases such as 'elephantiasis'."
"Okay, so you said you wanted to become a medical practitioner here, now I understand."
"It was October when I finally arrived in Batavia, my destination."
"Mr. Kaempfer, thank you for talking about your interesting story. I'm sure you'll be able to stay here for a while, first of all."
With that, Cleyer decided to end the long interview.

Today outside again, the rain was pouring down like water from a great waterfall. How can the sky produce so much rain?
The Governor-General had given advance notice of the meeting, Cleyer, Kaempfer and other key members of the East India Company staff had gathered in the conference room.

Cleyer, who was in a position to preside over the meeting, began by addressing everyone.

"I have received the company's policy, 'A New Strategy after the Ottoman Crisis', along with the details of the Ottoman siege of Vienna. I would like to explain this. Now I would like you to read this document."

With these words, Cleyer ordered the secretary to read it out.

The secretary began to read the document. It began with the rise of Turkey since the Middle Ages.

"In 1453, the Turkish Empire had attacked Constantinople, the capital of the Eastern Roman Empire, captured the fortress of the Knights of John on the island of Rhodes, gained control of the Mediterranean Sea, and was expanding its territory. In 1529, Sultan Süleyman I finally laid siege to Vienna, the Pearl of Europe. The Holy Roman Emperor at the time, Charles V, the leader of the House of Habsburg, called on all of Europe to come to his aid. The besieged resisted stubbornly. After a two-month siege, a sudden snowfall in October, too early to usher in winter, caused the Turks to retreat. The Turks were so surprised that they withdrew and Vienna was saved."

To Cleyer, who still remembered the Thirty Years' War, the European crisis seemed to be a religious war between peoples of different religions and a clash of different civilizations.

The secretary's reading continued.

"But in July 1683, the Turks again attacked Vienna, the heartland of the Habsburgs. The background was that Emperor Leopold I had refused to renew the 20-year peace treaty with Turkey. The Turkish army was led by the vizier Kara Mustafa Pasha who defied the orders of Sultan Mehmed IV, and surrounded the Vienna City Wall with 150,000 men. This was an expedition that aimed to make up for the failure of one hundred and fifty-four years earlier.

France, under the rule of Louis XIV, who had quickly established a centralized state, was in league with the Turks behind the scenes. The Turkish plan was to pinch off the Austrian capital, which had been weakened after the Thirty Years' War, through an alliance with France."

This French attitude was very strange to Cleyer. It seemed like an act of treachery to lend a helping hand to Turkey at a time of crisis in the European world. However, considering that Spain, which was behind France, was a member of the Habsburg family, it seemed to be a desperate measure for France's survival to help Turkey, which was trying to gain its stronghold.

The story was now approaching the climax of the siege.

"The Vienna garrison sent requests for help to European countries. The siege army had endured two months of bitter fighting. Then came the relief force of Catholic Allies with Pope Innocence XI, Holy Roman Emperor Leopold I, Archduke Charles V and King Sobieski of Poland.

Arriving at Kahlenberg, west of Vienna, the Allied forces engaged the Turks in a fierce battle that lasted twelve hours. Under the agreement that the King of Poland would take overall command of the Allied forces, the elite heavy cavalry of Sobieski moved in for a general assault. The Viennese siege army finally struck as well. Attacked from behind, the Turks were so disorganized that they broke the siege and ran away. The long and bitter battle was a victory for the Catholic allies in Europe.

From this moment on, Europe was freed from the long-standing Turkish nightmare. The Holy Roman Empire, led by Austria, regained its prestige and a flamboyant Baroque culture blossomed north of the Alps.

In order to meet the expanding demands of continental Europe in the wake of these dramatic changes, the East India Company had to increasingly strengthen and develop its functions.

As part of this, within Batavia's area of control, it must increase trade with Qing China, which is expanding its territory. Alongside this, the possibility of expanding trade with Japan, which has closed its eyes to world trends and continues to be closed off, obsessed with an outdated and narrow-minded idea of peace."

When Kaempfer finished listening, he realized that a new era had dawned.

The next day, almost around the same time in the afternoon, heavy rain began to fall again. The sound of the rain was huge and almost unbearable.

Cleyer and Kaempfer were talking together over a glass of palm juice. Together, they could talk carefree in their own national language. Cleyer spoke to him.

"By the way, about yesterday's talk. Where did you hear that the Turks had withdrawn from Vienna?"

"In Isfahan, Persia. It seems to have happened just as we were passing through Russian territory. How Europe managed to withstand was really amazing, wasn't it?"

"That's right. If Vienna had fallen, the world situation would have been very different.

It was truly a critical moment in world history."

The two men saw first-hand that Europe had moved on strongly after the crisis had passed.

"By the way, Mr. Kaempfer, about Japan in the company's new strategy."

Cleyer said to Kaempfer.

"I was the director of the Dutch trading factory on Dejima in

Nagasaki twice, from October 1682 to November the following year, and from November 1685 to October, the next year."

"Japan? I know about Japan, which Marco Polo long ago described as a 'golden country'. But that's all, I have no knowledge of it."

"I'm sure you don't. Then let me start from the beginning. The Portuguese and Spanish had already established themselves in Japan early on, but failed in their attempts to bring the country under the Catholic rule. The British and the Dutch then competed to establish trade links with Japan, and the Dutch won out. Japan was closed to foreign trade since 1639 and remained closed to the rest of the world. The only other country allowed in or out was Qing China."

Outside, it is still raining heavily. Kaempfer thought that at a time like this, the best thing to do is to listen to a long story.

Cleyer told him about the history of the Dutch trading factory on Dejima in Nagasaki.

"The first Dutch trading factory was opened in Hirado[6] in 1609. In 1637, after the Shimabara[7] Rebellion, the Edo Shogunate closed the country with a decree of seclusion, further strengthening the ban on Christian missionary work. On the orders of Shogun I'emitsu[8], the chief officer of police, Masashige Inoue, went to Hirado in 1640 to investigate the Dutch trading factory. He discovered that above the entrance to the warehouse, which had been built in 1639, the number of the Western calendar counting from the birth of Christ was inscribed.

He immediately ordered the demolition of all the buildings. In the West, the year of construction is sometimes indicated on the gables of newly built buildings, but either the architect in charge of the Dutch trading factory was careless or Masashige Inoue, who had noticed this, was slyer."

"The Japanese seem to be a very careful people who pay attention to the smallest details."

Kaempfer became interested in the Japanese.

"The following year, in 1641, François Caron, then director of the trading factory, complied with the demolition order, but he had no intention of leaving Japan. In 1613, the British had also opened a trading factory in Hirado, but had withdrawn from the island in 1623 after losing out in competition with the Dutch. The Dutch monopoly of trade had to be retained at all costs. Caron turned his attention to Dejima in Nagasaki, where the Portuguese had a base. This was an artificial island initially built to manage the Portuguese. It was built with the support of the Edo Shogunate and funded by influential Nagasaki locals, but was vacant at the time. The Portuguese paid an annual rent of 80 kan (approx. 300 kg, silver) for the land. Maximiliaan le Maire, the first head of the Dejima trading factory, concluded negotiations with them for 55 kan (approx. 206 kg, silver, about 250,000 euro in today's terms), and Dejima would remain the location of the Dutch trading factory for the next 215 years. When the trading factory in Hirado was closed, it must have been a real crisis. The old chief of the trading factory held out on the brink of losing a major interest, and the new chief of the trading factory was very clever in beating down the rent for the new location of Dejima."

"My hat is off to the East India Company for their shrewdness in recognizing Japan as an important trading partner."

"That's right. During my assignment in Nagasaki, I tried to systematically compile information on Japan and report it to the

---

6 An island, north-west of Nagasaki prefecture. In the 16th century there was a trading port with China, Portugal and Spain.

7 A revolt against the lord by farmers and Christians. (1637-38)

8 The third Shogun of the Tokugawa-clan.

head office."

Cleyer was a doctor and a first-class botanist.

"Trade with Japan was a lucrative business for the East India Company. It was also a great opportunity for me personally to make a fortune."

Cleyer looked back on this time while his gaze wandered into the distance.

"It was my second posting, when the head of the trading factory was given the privilege of illegal private trade. On landing, I wore the same kind of loose Chinese clothes as the predecessor, and I carried as many private trade goods as I could. I thought I was merely following precedent, but perhaps I went a little too far."

An official of the Nagasaki Magistrate's Office became suspicious of Cleyer's excessive methods and seized the scene of the smuggling. From then on, strict measures were taken to 'ban private trade'. As a result, he could no longer be posted to Nagasaki. The impact was not confined to him personally, but he also lost the great benefits the head of the trading factory could have expected from the Nagasaki trade.

"I might have done the same thing if that had been the custom."

Kaempfer consoled Cleyer.

"I will forever go down in Japanese records as an unfavorable Dutchman. In fact, I would have liked to have done more academically."

Cleyer's regret was great.

"So, there it is. Mr. Kaempfer, do you ever think of going to Japan? Japan remains a closed and unknown country. Following the policy of the head office, since yesterday I have been trying to open up trade with Japan. But I can no longer enter Japan."

These words sparked Kaempfer's curiosity. This is how Kaempfer who had no plans to go to Japan, developed an interest in the country. People generally want to do what they are forbidden to do, and want to see more and more what they are told they must not see. Kaempfer's interest may have been similar. But his decision was extremely fortunate for Japan and Europe.

"Dr. Cleyer, I am finally coming to Japan. I have a favor to ask you. What is the most important thing in Japan?"

When it became time to set sail, Kaempfer asked Cleyer.

Cleyer replied:

"Yes, that's right. Japanese is different from any other language. It is difficult to learn it in a short time. Therefore, in order to accurately understand the intentions of the Japanese, you need to find a good interpreter."

The dry season skies over Batavia were clear and the weather was perfect for embarkation.

On 7 May 1690, Kaempfer left Batavia aboard the sailing ship 'Waalstroom'. His curiosity was satisfied by a three-week stay in Ayutthaya, Siam (now Thailand), where he paid a courtesy call on the king.

Finally, he arrived in Nagasaki on 24 September. There, he stayed as a doctor in Dejima for about two years until August 1692. During this time, he made friends with Japanese Dutch interpreters Gonpachi Namura, Chinzan Narabayashi, Yozaemon Yokoyama, Ichirobei Baba and others, and recorded his extensive knowledge gained in Japan for posterity. However, one person who deserves special mention is his manager, Gen'emon Imamura. Kaempfer thoroughly trained this young Japanese in the Dutch language, making him his perfect right-hand man. Kaempfer thus made excellent use of Cleyer's advice. Kaempfer's valuable records, which are still held in the British Museum in London today, would probably not exist without Gen'emon Imamura. Kaempfer himself left many sketches, which provide a realistic picture of Japan at the time.

During his visit to Edo[9], Kaempfer had an audience with the fifth Shogun, Tsunayoshi. A souvenir of that trip was a large crab, which he took back to Europe as a specimen. This large crab was named after him 'Macroheira Kaempferi' and can still be seen today at the Witch Mayor Museum in his home town of Lemgo, Germany.

After two years in Japan, Kaempfer returned to The Netherlands on 6 October 1693 on the sailing ship 'Pampus' via South Africa. He was awarded a doctorate from Leiden University there and returned to his home town of Lemgo in 1694. Here he attempted to compile the results of his decade-long journey, but was too busy with his work as a doctor. This was compounded by the fact that he had a wife 30 years younger than himself.

It was not until 1712 that he was able to complete "Amoenitates Exoticae", a large book of 900 pages. The bulk of the book is devoted to Persia, with only a few mentions of Japan. In November 1716, Kaempfer passed away at the age of 65.

His inheritance and vast collection were passed on to his nephew, who sold it to Sir Hans Sloane, the British king's physician-in-charge, collector and inventor of recipes for cocoa drinks. The previously unpublished material on Japan was translated into English by the young Swiss physician Johann Kaspar Scheuchzer and published under the title 'the History of Japan' in 1727. It was translated into French and Dutch in 1729 and was later used as a guidebook for Thunberg's visits to Japan.

Queen Elizabeth II of the United Kingdom, who in 2012 celebrated 60 years on the throne, visited Japan for the first time in 1975.

In her speech at a banquet at the Imperial Palace, she quoted the words from the preface of 'the History of Japan'. Her speech began with the following words.

"Your Majesty,
I thank you warmly for your welcome and generous words about our country.
The Duke of Edinburgh and I are particularly glad to be in Japan. We remember with pleasure the visit that your Majesty and the Empress made to London in 1971, and our visit now sets a symbolic seal on the long continuity of association between our two countries.
The first British seafarers and traders who came to Japan during the time of Queen Elizabeth I, found much to wonder at and admire in your Japanese civilization. Later on 1727 an English translator of 'the History of Japan' wrote in his preface that the book described a valiant nation ... polite, industrious, virtuous people, enriched by a mutual commerce among themselves and possessed of a country on which nature hath lavished her most valuable treasures."
The preface of 'the History of Japan' that was published after Kaempfer's death, was quoted in Queen Elizabeth II's speech at the imperial palace, after he left Japan 283 years ago.
Queen Elisabeth I's reign lasted from 1558 to 1603. It was during this period that the Englishman William Adams and Dutchmen drifted ashore in Oita Prefecture on the Dutch ship, 'De Liefde', in April 1600.
William Adams later took the Japanese name Anjin Miura and served I'eyasu[10] Tokugawa as a samurai, ending his life in Japan.

9   Capital of Edo period
10 The first Shogun of the Tokugawa-clan

4. Africa

Thunberg spent Christmas that year with the Burmans. On the day before his departure Professor Burman called Thunberg into his study and handed him a document sealed in wax.

"I have a favor to ask you, Mr. Thunberg. It contains important information. But this will only make sense if you arrive safely in Japan. I cannot reveal the reason now, but I would like you to read it in Japan."

"I understand. I will open it when I arrive safely in Japan."

For him now, distant Japan was a far-off destination. His mind was now occupied with Africa, the first obstacle. So, wondering what this was about, Thunberg accepted it in silence.

The next day Thunberg embarked on his long journey, seen off by the Burmans. The sailing ship 'Schoonzigt' with him on board, left the port of Amsterdam on 30 December 1771. It was a typical gloomy winter day with light rain. The captain of this ship of the Dutch East India Company was the Swede, Rondecrantz. The fleet consisted of a number of vessels, with about one hundred sailors and nearly three hundred soldiers of the garrison on board, who were on their way to the Cape Governorate at the African Cape of Good Hope.

Following the same route, he had once taken to France, the ship passed through the Straits of Dover as the new year began. On board, a toast was raised to celebrate the New Year. Soon the port of Le Havre came into view in the haze on the left. By now our French friends must be celebrating the New Year with their friends and families.

From here onwards, the sea was unknown to Thunberg.

It had already been 275 years since the Portuguese Vasco da Gama set off on his first voyage to India in 1497. Although the art of navigation and the construction of ships had advanced considerably, the dangers were much the same as in the past. People had to live an anxious life on the stormy waters of the Atlantic.

The fleet had just passed the Brittany peninsula and entered the Bay of Biscay in Spain. It was the night of 4 January. A dish of crepes was served on the table of the ship on which Thunberg was staying. This dish was made of flour, rolled up with meat and vegetables and baked in the oven. The officers and the main crew, including Thunberg were sitting at the table together. He finished the meal as it was, although he thought the crepes tasted a little strange. The next morning, however, everyone who ate this meal suffered from severe stomach pains and diarrhea.

It was the first big test for Thunberg, who had embarked on a ship to cross the ocean with great ambition. Suffering from nausea and diarrhea, he had a high fever and was tormented by ominous dreams. The god of death with a large scythe, holding an hourglass in one hand, lured Thunberg to the underworld. The sands of the hourglass are drifting silently down, the light of life is just about to go out.

Suddenly he is snatched up by a great wave and tossed about in the ocean swell of a tempest. Barely out of the waves he pokes his head out and breathes heavily. Above the waves, the black cloaked figure of the God of Death appears again, beckoning to him. The sky is covered with black clouds and unnatural light shone through a gap in the clouds. Soon he sees himself walking around the quiet lakes and forests of his homeland. Then he hears his deceased father talking to him. His mother is also calling him loudly while her voice changes to the voice of Professor Linnaeus from Uppsala University. Then the figure of Professor Burman from Amsterdam suddenly appears. The professor shouts loudly at him. Nearby, his son Nicholas reaches out his hand and calls.

"Carl, do not fall down here. Do not die. Rouse your strength!"

How many times has Thunberg dreamt the same scene?

The call of Carl is replaced by Birgitta's voice.

"Do not die. Carl. I believe in you and I'm waiting for you. So please, live! Don't make me sad."

Thunberg reaches out his hand to Birgitta. She holds out her hand too. A great storm plays violently with her hair. Soon her warmth is felt in his hand. ...

As he passed through a pass of severe headaches and drowsiness, he recorded his symptoms in detail.

In the meantime, an investigation into the cause was carried out on board the ship and concluded that it was malignant food poisoning. The circumstances of the incident soon became clear.

On the night in question, in the ship's kitchen, the cook put flour into a bowl. However, he did not have enough and asked an apprentice to bring some flour from the ship's hold. He immediately went to the hold and returned with a bowl of flour. The cook stirred it with the flour in the cooking bowl and used it to bake the crepes. That was all there was to it. Then, what was it that the assistant brought?

It was lead white. This was the material added in paint that painters use to produce white colors. However, even if there was a painter on board, it is unlikely that the assistant brought the painting material from the hold of the ship. When lead white is heated, the color changes to red and becomes minium. This material was used to prevent corrosion of the ship's bottom. It was concluded that the assistant mistook it for flour. It was a major mishap caused by a small careless error. Fortunately, two months later, the symptoms of lead poisoning subsided and Thunberg recovered. His robust life force overcame the difficulties. However, his health was not completely restored and he suffered from the after effects.

The ship continued to sail. As they approached the equator, the temperature rose sharply and the heat, which Thunberg had never experienced before, set in. The blazing sun beat down mercilessly on deck. The sailors celebrated lively as they passed the equator. Eventually, the heat gradually subsided and the climate became more pleasant. The sky became clear and calm, like autumn back home, and the waves became quiet. Then a flat mountain came into view.

"That's the Table Mountain at the Cape of Good Hope."

The captain pointed to a mountain with a distinctive trapezoidal ridge in the distance. Over the mountain are superimposed clouds.

"We've finally arrived." Thunberg said, gazing at the mountain with emotion.

It was 16 April 1772.

When the sailing ship with him reached the Cape Governorate after a four-and-a-half-month voyage, half of the crew and passengers were ill, and the entire fleet had lost a hundred and ten men.

The job was no easy one, even for Thunberg, who was experiencing his first practicing as a doctor.

Eventually, the ship entered the bay gliding lightly. The docks were packed with a large number of East India Company officials and locals. The sails were lowered and Thunberg unloaded his luggage from the vessel. As he disembarked, the captain smiled and shook hands with the acting governor-general, Joachim van Plettenberg. The captain introduced Thunberg. The acting governor-general shook Thunberg's hand firmly and spoke.

"Welcome to the Cape Governorate. I was told of your arrival by my predecessor, Governor-General Tulbagh. Unfortunately, he passed away a few months ago. I have had to act in his place at short notice." Thunberg was shocked by these words, right at his arrival. He had brought with him a letter of recommendation from Professor Linnaeus to the Governor-General. Governor Tulbagh was supposed to be an active supporter of the Cape Governorate's expeditions into the interior. He was so interested in and knowledgeable about botany that he himself sent Professor Linnaeus rare African plants. It was a surprise to learn that such a trustworthy potential patron was no longer with us. With the exception of people like Governor Tulbagh, the East India Company's employees were usually not interested in academic matters, as their main objective was to make a profit.

There is nothing more disheartening than coming to an unknown place and not seeing the people you counted on.

"We are planning a welcome party at the Governor-General's office this evening to celebrate your arrival. We will take you to your accommodation so that you can first relax after your long journey." With these words, van Plettenberg gave instructions to a young employee at his side.

On either side of the Governor-General's building, which was built facing the sea, were rows of Dutch style houses. Behind them were farmlands. Thunberg felt as if he had arrived in some Dutch village. Adjacent to the farmland was meadow with lots of long-horned cattle. One of the farmhouse-style buildings was set aside as Thunberg's accommodation. Next to it was a hospital building with an infirmary and wards.

The welcome party that night was a success. The people were kind to the young doctor, newly arrived from his home country. The acting governor-general welcomed the visitors.

"I would like to extend a hearty welcome to all of you here at the Cape Governor's Office. I am sure that the voyage has been full of hardships. I offer my deepest condolences to those who lost their lives."

Upon hearing these words, everyone stood up and prayed silently. The welcome party was a ceremony of mourning for those who had passed away as well as a moment of sharing joy with the sailors who arrived alive. When he saw that everyone was seated, he continued speaking.

"Let me give you a brief history of this place. The East India Company was established in 1602 and fifty years later in 1652, the Governor-General's Office was opened here, exactly one hundred and twenty years ago. The first Governor-General was Jan van Riebeeck, who held the position for ten years. During this period, the company continued to develop with great achievements and huge profits. It is needless to say that its main trade was in spices from Java.

Prior to the establishment of the Cape Governorate, the Company was based in Batavia, Java, in 1619, but had also established a trading factory on Hirado island, Japan, ten years earlier."

It seemed strange to Thunberg, who had heard this story, that the bases in Batavia and Japan had been opened long before the Cape Governorate in order to gradually develop the East Indian trade.

Van Plettenberg's speech continued.

"The role of the Cape Governor-General's Office has been extremely important in the history of the company up to the present day. Located halfway between the mainland and Batavia, it was an essential strategic supply base. In the Indian Ocean, a strong southwesterly monsoon blows from April to September in the winter, which acts as a tailwind and carries ships to Batavia. Conversely, in the summer months of November through March, the northeast monsoon is strong, and ships loaded with goods from Asia call at the Cape Governor's Station."

His story was long, but it gave Thunberg a good understanding of the existence of the Cape Governorate. The acting governor also spoke about the natives who lived in the area.

"The people who lived here were called Khoikhoi, and their main occupation was cattle breeding. At first, we bartered with them for water and food, but this was no longer sufficient as the number of ships coming and going increased. Therefore, it became necessary for us to cultivate our own farmland and to organize and efficiently manage our livestock. No need to mention how important it is to supply water, vegetables, and wine to the ships bound for India. Today, we have a huge harvest here."

That evening, the welcome banquet featured a sumptuous meal with local wine, fresh beef, vegetables, and fruits, surpassing the cuisine of the home country.

A few days later, a Swedish East India Company fleet arrived in the port. On board the ship was a fellow student of Thunberg's. He was unexpectedly reunited with Anders Sparrman, who had studied at the Uppsala University.

"I had no idea you were coming here, I'm so glad we both survived the voyage."

Thunberg hugged his friend out of sheer joy.

"I think it was while you were in Paris that the idea of going to Africa suddenly came up to me. I was lucky enough to be chosen and sent."

Sparrman told the story of how it all happened.

The joy of their reunion must have been indescribable. The excitement of their reunion, however, was short-lived. The two men soon became rivals, and a sense of competition sparked between them.
Sparrman had a clear reason for coming to the Cape Governorate by a different route. It was a sense of competition with the British and the Dutch, which was a matter of Swedish pride. This was reflected in the competition within the Uppsala University. At the same time, even The Netherlands were exposed to great risk, and it was a rational idea to cover the risk.
The Swedish East India Company was established in Gothenburg on the west coast of Sweden in 1731, 129 years later than the Dutch one, and was the largest Swedish company of the 18th century. The company was initially operated with a term of fifteen years. The articles of incorporation were revised in 1746, 1766, and 1786, before closing the curtain on its history in 1813. The late company had already made agreements with the Dutch and British trading posts, which had a long history, and was allowed to use their bases.
The month of April was winter when Thunberg arrived, and during that time, he pondered the destination of his spring expedition and who to assign as his assistant. During these days, Thunberg found Johann Andreas Auge, a gardener with the East India Company, to be the most suitable collaborator for him. Judging from his name, he was probably German. One day Thunberg approached him.
"Mr. Auge, I came here mainly to study African plants. I have heard that you are an expert on the local situation. Would you be willing to accompany me in my research?"
"I have already been into the interior of the country. I myself am interested in continuing my research and would be happy to join you."
"I would appreciate it very much. So where should we make our

spring exploration destinations?"

Auge began by explaining the situation in detail.

"The area around the Cape Governorate is safe and secure. However, it is not exaggerated to say that once you step into the interior, you are in danger. The purpose of the Dutch was to establish a peaceful transit base for the Asian route through trade with the natives. However, achieving this goal was not easy. The natives were not eager to supply the Dutch with the foodstuffs they needed."

His explanation convinced him.

No people desire new changes if they live a peaceful and satisfying life. When that happens, the Dutchman's next move is obvious.

"The Dutch drove the natives away and converted their settlements to farmland. The nomadic Khoikhoi joined forces with the San, who lived as hunter-gatherers in the mountains and semi-desert regions of the interior and fought back. The Dutch had no choice but to respond. Numerous immigrants came from Europe. For example, many Protestant Huguenots from France, who had been driven out of their country by the Reformation, settled in the region. These Europeans expanded their own agricultural and pasturelands toward the interior of Africa, and the conflict with the indigenous people has been repeated."

"I see. then, let's say that our first expedition will be to an area that is not too dangerous and unknown to the Europeans."

A few days later, Auge put his plan on a map and explained it to Thunberg.

"From the Cape, we will first reach Saldanha, 100 kilometers to the northwest, and then turn around and go southeast to Swellendam, about 240 kilometers. From there, the route continues eastward until it reaches the Gamtoos River, which flows into the Indian Ocean and forms the border of Dutch territory 400 kilometers away. The total distance is 1330 kilometers, but the area is relatively safe and free from conflict with the current inhabitants."

The expedition was set to begin on September 7, 1772. Thunberg intended to be well prepared by then. At the same time, he was well aware that his final destination would be Japan. Japan had no diplomatic relations with anyone other than The Netherlands, and all Europeans visiting Japan were Dutch, so there was no way to communicate with them except through Dutch interpreters. Therefore, Thunberg decided to master the Dutch language during his stay in the Cape Governorate.

On their first expedition, Thunberg and Auge rode horses and transported their equipment with an oxcart. It was spring in the southern hemisphere, the ideal season for plant growth. Thunberg, in his element, ventured into the ocean of the plant world as he had never seen it before. The expedition was well underway. He returned safely to the Cape Governorate on January 2 of the following year, as scheduled. It was just a year after he had left Amsterdam. He immediately spent his days compiling the materials he had collected and writing his thesis. At that time, he received a happy letter from his hometown. It was a letter from the old Professor Linnaeus.

"Dr. Thunberg, congratulations. The University of Uppsala has decided to confer on you the degree of Doctor of Medicine in June 1772.

It is with great pleasure that I write this letter. I am glad to hear that you have regained your health after the great mishap you had on the voyage to Cape Governorate. I am sure that by the time this letter reaches you, the first results of your African expedition will have been obtained. I am cheering you on from Uppsala as you realize my dream. I hope that you will continue to take good care of yourself and to do good work."

Reading this letter, Thunberg could not help being moved to tears of joy.

After the report of the first expedition was compiled, Thunberg began preparing for the second expedition without a break. This time Auge was unable to accompany him because he was returning home. Fortunately, an Englishman, Francis Masson, came forward. "Dr. Thunberg, my specialty is botany and I am also a gardener. I came to the Cape Governorate on a commission from Kew Gardens in London to collect plants from the Portuguese island of Madeira and Africa in the Atlantic Ocean. Moreover, I know Professor Linnaeus very well. We exchange letters from time to time."

He, too, had been on major expeditions and was a good match for Thunberg. But he was not familiar with local conditions.

"Mr. Masson, it is very encouraging to have an experienced person like yourself accompanying me on my expedition. We have a lot of unfinished business from last year's expedition. We don't need to change much from last year's route, but I would like to incorporate some different paths in parts."

"That's fine. Let's hear your suggestions first."

"As last year, we will go northwest from the Cape to Saldanha, then northeast through Citrusdal to Swellendam, where we went last year. From there, we will turn east and cross the Gamtoos River, which we also turned back to last year, and continue on to Port Elizabeth. It will be a major expedition, covering a total distance of 1600 kilometers round trip."

"I have no objection to that route."

"I also would like to reach the summit of Mount Winterhoek, which rises 2000 meters above sea level. What do you think?"

"It will be a deadly adventure. Let's give it a try."

The two prepared themselves and set out on September 11, the same time as last year. This time, they crossed the border of the Cape Colony to Port Elizabeth and reached the Sundays River in the north. However, their horses and oxen were too weak to continue the expedition any further.

They returned to the Cape on January 29, 1774.

He and Masson planned Thunberg's third expedition.

"Dr. Thunberg, why don't we take the plunge this time and concentrate on the northern part of the Cape?"

"That would certainly be interesting. It is truly uncharted territory for us."

He agreed to the proposal and quickly formulated a concrete plan the next day.

"First of all, we will go north from the Cape for about 300 kilometers to the Hantam Mountains. From there, we would head southeast through Roggeveld and back to the Cape Governorate on a relatively short, but still three-month research expedition of 700 kilometers, what do you think?"

"I have no objection to that Dr. Thunberg."

The departure was on September 29, 1974, and the return was on December 29.

Such an adventure into the unknown was not accomplished without any difficulty. Thunberg's financial base was perilous, and at times he suffered from the 'money shortage disease'.

"Dear Professor Burman,

The valuable specimens collected during our two expeditions to the Cape will be sent to Amsterdam on the next ship. Fortunately, I have been blessed with competent and kind partners, overcome many dangers and achieved great results. However, the scholarship from Uppsala University has run out and the funds given to me by volunteers in Amsterdam have also been exhausted. With the advance payment from my company for a part-time surgeon, there is no way for me to go on another expedition. Therefore, I would like to ask you for a little more financial support."

The Burmans were astonished when they received this letter and informed Professor Linnaeus of Thunberg's financial plight. Thanks to their efforts, Thunberg received a further scholarship from Uppsala University. Professor Burman's son, Nicholas, sent letters of encouragement to Thunberg, believing him all the way in spite of his father's pessimism that the expedition would fail. One can only imagine how much this warm support encouraged Thunberg.

Thus, Thunberg's 'Natural History of South Africa' still retains its value to this day.

After three adventurous trips during his three-year stay in the Cape Governorate, Thunberg decided to move on to his next destination, Batavia. On March 2, 1775, with the southeasterly monsoon, Thunberg sailed once again as a 'part-time surgeon' aboard the East India Company's sailing ship, the 'Loo,' bound for Batavia. It was fortunate for him that the Indian Ocean was calm. He did not have to risk his life as he had done in the past on Atlantic voyages. After only a month's voyage, he reached Batavia, the East India Company's base on the island of Java.

5. Japan

As the sailing ship carrying Thunberg approached the harbor, the town of Batavia was in full view. The town was dominated by a spire reminiscent of a Dutch castle, with the Dutch flag waving at the peak. The town measures 1400 meters from north to south and 1000 meters from east to west, and the only gate is on the city wall. He was escorted to the governor's building and received a warm welcome from the governor, van der Parra. Here too, Professor Burman's letter of recommendation to the Governor was of great help.

"How was your cruise, Dr. Thunberg?"

The Governor asked.

"The vast and boundless sea of the Indian Ocean was like being placed in the infinity of space, with no sense of time."

Thunberg replied frankly.

"You are right. The ships of the East India Company have been sailing on that vast ocean for one hundred and seventy years."

The governor's words gave Thunberg a glimpse of the hardships of his predecessors. The governor explained the history of Batavia to him in detail.

"When the Dutch East India Company gained control of these waters, they decided to use Batavia as a base from which to efficiently organize trade in East Asia. In other words, they made Batavia function as their headquarters. All ceramics from China, spices from the Moluccas Islands northeast of Java and many other things were traded and settled here. In other words, the trade structure of the company was such that transactions were completed in Asia, with little negative impact on the economy of The Netherlands. After 1665, Ceylon (now Sri Lanka) also became a base for the East India Company. In contrast, the British East India Company is controlled directly by the parent company in London, which is the big difference between the two companies."

 In today's terms, it is The Netherlands that gave the local company the settlement function to speed up the decision-making process, and the United Kingdom that kept the authority of the head office in the home country and made the local company a branch office.

The Governor's explanation was easy for Thunberg to understand. The Governor continued.

"The spices and cotton brought to Europe by the East India Company were enormously profitable. The problem was that the people of India and Asia were not very interested in European products. The Indian and Asian countries mainly demanded precious metals such as gold, silver, and copper in exchange for their products. Over time, therefore, precious metals from Europe were lost to the rest of the world, causing serious economic problems. In this sense, it was to the advantage of the Dutch East India Company that Japan initially offered silver and copper in exchange for the overseas products of The Netherlands. Even today, Japan exports copper bars of excellent purity."

Thunberg recalled something Professor Burman had once told him. "But even in Japan, the annual trade volume is limited to prevent the outflow of precious metals, correct?"

"That is correct. You know this very well, don't you? You are going to Japan, aren't you? This autumn, Nagasaki will have a rotating post of head of a trading factory called 'Captain'. Here is Mr. Feith, who will accompany you. Let me introduce him to you."

The Governor said and ordered his servant to call Mr. Feith. Soon after, the new head of the trading house appeared and welcomed Thunberg.

"Pleased to meet you. Dr. Thunberg. We will be going to Japan together, and I am looking forward to working with you. I have already served as director of the trading factory two years ago. This will be my third time."

Tall, blond, and a typical Dutch gentleman was the first impression this captain made on Thunberg. When he smiled, there was a familiarity that would put any stranger at ease. To be respected by one's peers and to be approachable to foreigners would have been the first requirement for the Captain.

"I see. You are an expert on Japan. I see that you will be spending a year in Japan with me. It is my pleasure to meet you."

They clasped each other's hands tightly.

"Why do you keep going back to Nagasaki? It seems to me that it takes a lot of courage to risk a dangerous voyage to Japan."

Feith replied.

"In the past, trade with Japan was very profitable. But then the Japanese government, the Edo Shogunate, began to impose more severe trade restrictions, and Captain must be changed every year. Japan is a very special country, and people cannot come and go freely from the small artificially built island of Dejima. Only once a year, one had to make the long journey to the capital city of Edo to seek an audience with the Shogun.

They cannot go directly to Edo by ship, nor are they allowed to use horses. They had to go on foot in a procession. It is such an inconvenient country, and the only way to continue the connections I have made with the Japanese is to be posted to Japan every other year. But that is not all. For some reason, I love Japan and Japanese people. I have witty and enterprising friends there."

Hearing this, Thunberg was reassured that the contents of Kaempfer's book was basically unchanged eighty-five years later. However, he did not know the reason why the head of the trading factory, Captain Feith, was so pro-Japanese.

Governor van der Parra felt relieved that the two men seemed to be getting along well. Then he asked,

"By the way, Dr. Thunberg, you have some time before leaving for Japan. How do you spend this time?"

"I am preparing to leave for Japan, but I would also like to see around Java a little bit."

Although he answered, he had a hard time adjusting to the tropical climate. While in the Cape, he led an active and hardworking life, making the most of his time and compiling as many reports as possible, but here it was different. Most of the Dutch stationed at the Governorate led a life of idleness and laziness, so to speak. For some reason, he too, was not energetic. The climate was too harsh for Europeans.

The inhabitants of the Governorate of Batavia were a handful of Europeans, followed by locals, and the overwhelming majority were Chinese. Thunberg even felt that Batavia was somehow a Chinese town. This was understandable if it was the Chinese who were involved in the trade of goods sought by the Dutch.

When he arrived in Batavia, Thunberg had made up his mind not to repeat the impoverished life he had led in South Africa, in Japan. Until then, Dutch members posted to Japan had engaged in some form of private trade and had earned a reasonable amount of personal profit. He also, decided to look into the situation. Eventually, a Chinese merchant who frequented the Governorate approached him with an offer to buy goods that would make him a great profit if he went to Japan. It was a unicorn tusk. Thunberg had heard of this animal in European legends, but had never actually seen one until then.

This Asian animal, however, is a rare species called 'narwhal', a single-tusked animal with deformed teeth that lives in the Arctic Ocean, and its tusks are prized in Japan as an energizer in Chinese medicine and sold for a high price. Thunberg refused to buy the commodity for the exorbitant amount of money the merchant was asking, but finally broke down at the insistence of the Chinese man, who was eager to lower his price. He wondered if the Chinese had the gene of business spirit in them since time immemorial. It did not suit his character to go into debt to get the 'narwhal' tusk, since the initial price was halved. Thunberg had borrowed money to acquire it.

The ship's departure for Japan was set for June 20, making it impossible to conduct a large-scale survey in the two months before the ship's departure. Thunberg attempted a short expedition to Bogor, 60 km south of Batavia. The distance was not a problem based on his experience in Africa, but the tropical climate made it difficult. He also took a ship to Semarang, 400 km to the east. He would have liked to visit the Moluccas Islands, a spice-producing region 2500 km northeast of Batavia, where the East India Company had earned most of its profits in the past, but this was not possible.

Thunberg boarded the sailing ship 'Stavenisse' from Batavia to Nagasaki as scheduled. During the voyage, Thunberg had the status of senior surgeon. The somewhat smaller and slower ship 'Bleijenburg' accompanied her. As the Chinese mainland came into view, the accompanying ship was hit by a storm that snapped one mast after another, rendering the voyage impossible. The ship had no choice but to seek rescue in the port of Macau, and had to be repaired in the port of Canton. The voyage to Japan was thus cancelled, and the entire cargo of sugar was destroyed. Sugar was a valuable product that brought a high profit in trade with Japan, and the loss, incurred by the East India Company due to the shipwreck, was enormous.

The voyage to the East China Sea reminded Thunberg of his former nightmare in the Atlantic. The journey to Japan is recorded as one of the most difficult in the history of the East India Company. But he had already experienced the storms of the sea when he sailed the Atlantic to Africa. Moreover, at that time, he was wandering on the border between life and death due to the lead poisoning. Compared to that, he was confident that he could overcome this storm as long as he was in good health.

The 'Stavenisse' passed along Formosa (now Taiwan) and arrived safely at the port of Nagasaki, as he had expected. Five years had already passed since his departure from home. How moved he was when he finally reached Japan. Looking west into the sky, he spoke to his former professors, Linnaeus and Burman.

"I have finally arrived in Japan. It has been a long journey. I am grateful for the blessings of the two of you. I will do my best to meet your expectations here."

When the ship anchored in Nagasaki harbor in the early morning of August 13, a signal fire rose from the nearby mountains to announce the arrival of the Dutch ship. It was the 'watchman' of the Nagasaki Magistrate's Office. Soon after, a small boat approached and officials boarded the Dutch ship.

Feith, the head of the trading factory said to Thunberg:

"The long and tedious inspection of the cargo is about to begin. After that rigorous inspection, all the cargo will be brought ashore in small boats."

The goods imported to Japan by the Dutch included sugar, ivory, tin, lead, chintz, and Dutch fabrics. These imported goods were auctioned at the market held at Dejima. The equivalent was not paid in cash. A kind of draft was drawn.

Captain who was already familiar with the procedure and the work involved, said calmly,

"When the ship's cargo is unloaded, Japanese export goods will be loaded."

The goods included copper, camphor, kimonos, ceramics, soy sauce, and sake, all of excellent quality. The copper was brought to India and traded there at a very good price.

On October 14, two months after her arrival, the "Stavenisse," returning to Batavia, was towed to Takaboko-jima island at the entrance to Nagasaki bay. There it again dropped anchor.

Feith sympathized with the frustrated Thunberg and said, "Next, the Dutch stationed at Dejima will be replaced."

At this time, Thunberg felt like a prisoner on a motionless ship. He was caught in a stifling sense of entrapment, deprived of his freedom. It was a reaction to his high expectations of Japan as his final destination. He had been born to run around in the fields and mountains. He wrote frankly to Nicholas Burman in Amsterdam about his agonizing feelings at this time.

"Nagasaki, October 1, 1775

Dear Nicholas,

I have finally arrived in Japan, my final destination. Considering the long process, I have traveled so far, I think we have arrived well on this small island. All the hardships I had to go through up to now were only preparations for coming to this country. But what I felt when I arrived here was isolation and a sense of hopeless anxiety about the future..."

But Thunberg was not a man to stay blocked up forever. Although the sailing vessel was under constant surveillance, he was likely to be able to take a small boat out to one of the surrounding islets to relax. Thunberg was not about to let this opportunity pass by idly. He quickly made friends with an interpreter dispatched by the Nagasaki Magistrate's Office and immediately offered to collect plants. Although he had only been there a short time, he was able to land on Takaboko-jima island and discover some rare plants. This small success gave him great confidence.

A few weeks after anchoring in the shade of Takaboko-jima island, the change of the Dutch members took place in early November. The 'Stavenisse', carrying the letter addressed to Nicholas Burman, returned for Batavia. The fourteen newly appointed Europeans were left on the narrow island of Dejima.

The Dutch on Dejima consisted of people from various European countries. However, as long as they spoke Dutch as a common language and interacted with Japanese interpreters, they were all understood as Dutch by the Japanese, no matter what their nationality was. Kaempfer was German, Thunberg was Swedish, and von Siebold, who later came to Nagasaki, was also German. The people on board the East India Company's vessels would have been of many different nationalities and backgrounds.

But life on Dejima was a prison for Thunberg. He was forbidden to leave the island freely and could not keep abreast of what happened in the world. His sense of entrapment never lifted as he explored the land of Africa like a flapping wing. Moreover, in both Africa and Batavia, Thunberg was provided with housing in the Dutch style, and his lifestyle was no different from that in Europe.

The house assigned to him was the second house straight ahead from the entrance of Dejima and turned right at the first corner.

There were three small, neat rooms and a storage. He said to Feith, "Why should we live in a Japanese-style dwelling? There are much more comfortable houses being built in the Cape and Batavia."

"I understand your feelings well, but we have no choice because of the contract with the Shogunate. All we can do is to remodel an entrance and a viewing platform on the roof."

"I see what you mean. The entrance of the Captain's house has an unusual design, but is that your taste?"

"No, it is not. I don't know whose taste it was, but I'm sure it was the head of the Dutch trading factory who was nostalgic for the drawbridges over the canals in Holland and made them look like that."

"It's getting a little chilly these days, isn't it? I'm used to the cold in Sweden, but the drafts that blow in are a bit annoying."

"After a while, we begin with using charcoal fires to keep warm, but the Nagasaki Magistrate's Office is very nervous when it comes to handling fire. There have been fires in the past, and each time the rules have become stricter."

"I am not financially able to afford it, but I know quite a few of them who manage to live comfortably with the furniture and decorating materials they bring themselves."

Thunberg was not interested in such things, fortunately or unfortunately.

There were also bread bakers in Nagasaki who delivered freshly baked bread to Dejima. There was a Dutch cook living on Dejima who prepared Dutch cuisine. There were also locals brought in from Batavia, creating a truly international atmosphere. The Dutch played billiards in a building built on the southeast side of the island, while the Batavians enjoyed badminton. Dejima is also the birthplace of badminton in Japan.

Soon after, the year was over and the New Year came. The morning was cold, but no snow fell. The officials of the Nagasaki Magistrate's Office and other important people in Nagasaki, dressed in formal attire, came to greet the New Year at the house of the director, known as the 'Captain's Room'. At noon, the guests were invited to a formal dinner in the hall. In Japan at that time, the 'Captain's Room' was the only banquet hall where one could taste European food. It was, so to speak, 'the Open Dejima' of the New Year.

As they all took their places at the large dining table, Feith offered his New Year's greetings and the Nagasaki Magistrate's Office's director expressed his gratitude. Soon the soup was served to everyone's plates by the waiter. All the invited Japanese tasted it. However, no one took a bite of the meat dish, cakes, or cookies that followed. At the end of the banquet, surprisingly, nothing was left at all. The food was placed on plates and covered with a piece of paper with the name of the Dutchman from the trading factory who had sent it to the city of Nagasaki. This was repeated several times.

When Thunberg saw this, he was surprised and asked Feith, who was seated next to him.

"What on earth has happened?"

"This is just one of the New Year's rituals," he said, "to give as many Japanese as possible a chance to taste something they normally can't have. The meat is dried and seems to be used in Chinese medicine."

Thunberg was convinced.

In the afternoon, Japanese food was served out. The courtesans of 'Maruyama', invited by the Captain, served warmed sake for everyone and celebrated the New Year with a lively New Year's dance performance. As the evening stars began to twinkle, the invited guests left.

The festivity full of surprises was over. Thunberg also returned to his house and found himself alone in the evening silence. In the chilling solitude, he remembered Christmas three years ago at the Burman's house in Amsterdam. Their warmth and gentleness made him miss them inexplicably. Nothing reminds one more of his hometown and the people close to him than spending Christmas and New Year in an alien country. It was then that Thunberg remembered Professor Burman's letter, which had been tucked away deep in his luggage. He took it out and opened the seal. It read as follows:

"Amsterdam, December 26, 1772

Dear Mr. Thunberg,

When you open this letter in Japan, I will have to call you Doctor. Let me congratulate you on your safe arrival in Japan. The reason I entrusted you with my letter in the first place is due to confidential requests from persons of noble rank.

They are Friedrich August III of Saxony, King George III of England, and Empress Maria Theresa of Habsburg, the Holy Roman Empire's ally in Vienna. You will be surprised. All of these European political leaders are asking for 'Japanese Camellia' and each of them sent their requests to me through different channels. This was probably a coincidence, but it was also completely unexpected.

The first was Friedrich August III of Saxony. The request came to me through the Dutch Minister in Dresden. The king has such a deep knowledge of plants that he is known as 'the reigning Gardener on the throne'. Pillnitz's current garden is a true reflection of his taste. Perhaps it was his strong interest in Japanese camellias that led to his decision to get the plant in the first place.

As you probably know, King George III of England has been reigning since his great-grandfather's reign from Hanover, Germany. His great-grandfather and grandfather spent more time in their hometown of Hanover than in London during their reign. Their castle was called Herrenhausen, and their gardens were maintained by Johannes Busch and Conrad Loddiges, two of the finest court gardeners in the world.

They came to England by order of King George II and ran a successful horticultural business in the suburbs of London. I knew Loddiges personally, and he was the one who informed me of George III's intentions. He wanted one camellia each for Herrenhausen in Hanover and for Kew Garden in London.

Finally, the Habsburgs in Vienna; an envoy from Vienna visited me in secret. The Habsburgs survived the War of Succession with Prussia, and their imperial consort, Maria Theresa, reigned as the de facto empress of the Holy Roman Empire. When an empress or queen is ruling a country, there are relatively few wars, and the economy and culture flourish. Vienna also has the stunning gardens of Schönbrunn, and the palace is a blooming center of Baroque culture.

I don't know why they need a living Japanese camellia, but it seems to have something to do with porcelain. Saxony is the home to Meissen porcelain, the first European porcelain invented. His great-grandfather, August the Strong, had Böttger create this brand. In Herrenhausen, there is the Hanoverian porcelain kiln 'Fürstenberg', and in England, there is Wedgwood, which is not porcelain. In Vienna, there is Augarten porcelain, which was leaked from Meissen. I imagine that the purpose of this project is to develop some new pottery with a design based on the camellia flower motif. For this purpose, they need a live camellia. As I showed you, there is a beautiful camellia on an Arita-yaki jar in my house. It may have originated in Dresden, but the information may have been passed on to London and Vienna.

These are all the requests that came to me. Therefore, Dr. Thunberg, while you are in Japan, I would like you to obtain camellias and send them to Europe. The king of each country may know that the same request has come to me from each other. In that case, it might be bad for my position if the camellia is of a different kind. People can see well what others have. Therefore, I would like them to be of the same kind.

I hope that your stay in Japan will be fruitful and that you will return safely to Holland and show your good health at home with the Japanese camellias.

Prof. Johannes Burman"

Thunberg immediately began to ponder. If he could freely roam the fields, mountains, and towns of Japan, obtaining camellias would not be a problem. Camellias had been a common plant in Nagasaki since these days.

Dutch interpreters often visited Thunberg on Dejima. They were eager to acquire new European knowledge, especially about medicine. Among them was Kosaku Yoshio, who was so fluent in Dutch that he became a first-class interpreter at a young age, and was so knowledgeable and studious that he was now an authority in his own right. Thunberg got along well with him. The year before Thunberg arrived in Nagasaki, 'Kaitai Shinsho' (New Text on Human Anatomy) by Genpaku Sugita and Ryotaku Maeno was published. The two men had received guidance from Kosaku Yoshio in translating the book from Dutch, and he had written the preface to the book.

One day in spring, Kosaku Yoshio together with Setsu'emon and his son, Den'nosuke Shige, both interpreters as well, came to visit Thunberg and said,

"These two men have a deep knowledge of plants, and I am sure you will get along well with them."

Thunberg began talking with them, showing them plant specimens that he had collected on Takaboko-jima Island during his arrival at the Nagasaki port. What they said was spot-on and Thunberg's trust in them grew rapidly.

"By the way, Mr. Shige, are there any camellias blooming outside Dejima?"

Setsu'emon Shige replied.

"Yes, they have begun to bloom. Camellias are the flower that heralds the coming of spring, and their beauty is exceptional. It is quite natural if you would like to see camellia flowers in this small island of Dejima. I have heard that there are no camellias in Europe."

Thunberg nodded and continued.

"I would like to get my hands on some of those camellias."

Setsu'emon Shige considered and said,

"I know someone who is in the plant business. Why don't you pay him a visit the next time you are allowed out?"

Thunberg said happily.

"Thank you, Mr. Shige, that's very kind of you. I will ask the magistrate for permission to go out and collect plants. Where would you like to go?"

"About twelve kilometers northeast of Dejima, there is a village called 'Koga'. There are many people who run nurseries there for a long time, and they grow many rare plants."

A few days later, Thunberg, accompanied by Setsu'emon Shige and other interpreters, went to the outskirts of Nagasaki to gather plants. It was a glorious day, still a little early for spring. In the village, bush warblers were singing beautifully. Thunberg's body and soul seemed to be filled with joy having freedom in a long time. Setsu'emon Shige led him to a nursery where numerous saplings of cherry, plum, maple and pine trees were planted on a gentle slope. A good-natured nursery man spoke to Thunberg as he led the visitors.

"Would you like camellias, sir? I have an area planted only camellias right over there, so you can choose the one you like best."

He led them to a place where camellias of various kinds had been planted and were in full bloom in a variety of colors.

White, red, pink, and white with red stripes, it was a gorgeous sight that Thunberg had never seen before.

After taking a look around, Thunberg said.

"I like that camellia, red, a little pink. I can't describe its simple but lovely beauty."

"This is a type of camellia called 'yabutsubaki', and it grows wild everywhere, but the one on the island of Gotō in Nagasaki is famous. There are trees over many hundred years old, and I brought these shrubs from the island."

"If it is such a long-lived camellia, it will survive the long voyage to Europe and bloom for a long time in the land where it has taken root. I will choose this camellia."

When Thunberg said this, a young girl carrying a bamboo basket, appeared from behind a camellia sapling. When she saw Thunberg, she took off her indigo-dyed headdress and greeted him. The nurseryman said:

"This is my daughter, Hana. I let her help me tend the saplings and squeeze the camellia oil."

The girl's hair was black, and her eyes were equally black by a sparkling light. Her face is fair and her crimson lips make it stand out even more.

Thunberg stared at the young girl in silence for a moment, feeling as if a camellia incarnation had appeared before him. He, for a while, lost himself in the mysterious beauty he had never seen before.

Eventually, as if awakening from a dream, he smiled at the girl.
"Is your name Hana?"
Setsu'emon Shige interpreted.
"My name is Hana."
The girl answered shyly.
"Hana? Does 'hana' mean flower?"
Thunberg asked Setsu'emon Shige.
"That is correct, you have already learned Japanese."
Hearing this, people burst into laughter.
"It is difficult to take these camellias to Dejima right now. Soon, it is time to go to Edo with the Captain. Could you keep it here for a while?"
"I will. Until then, let my daughter take good care of it."
When her father said this, Hana nodded her head shyly.

  A few days later, Kosaku Yoshio, the chief interpreter, visited Thunberg on Dejima.
"I congratulate you on finding a camellia that you like"
he said and asked him.
"But I don't quite understand why you want four of the same camellias. ..."
"I don't know the details myself, please don't ask me any further. But it is a request from an influential person in Amsterdam. By the way, Mr. Yoshio, I have something unusual for you."
What he showed him was a 'narwhal tusk'.
When Kosaku Yoshio saw it,
"Well, it is not ivory, but what could it be?"
Thunberg said casually.
"It is the tusk of a narwhal that lives in the Arctic Ocean."
The Dutch trade expert stared at the tusk in amazement.

"There is a record that it was brought to Dejima a long time ago. It is also said that Hideyoshi Toyotomi[11] had a narwhal ornamental hairpin."

Thunberg nodded. There was no way that the words of a scholar as erudite as Thunberg could be false. Kosaku Yoshio was known at the time as a wealthy scholar as well as a great interpreter.

He asked,

"Doctor, would you be so kind as to sell this to me?"

Although he was aware that this was private trade against the official rule, valuable items often came to Japan through this route.

This was how Thunberg was able to make an unexpectedly large sum of money.

Sensing Thunberg's unexpected interest in business, Kosaku Yoshio turned the conversation to the economic side of things. Thunberg's answer was quite interesting.

"I have traveled through Africa and Batavia, but never before have I been in a country where commerce is as advanced as in Japan, and where the currency is widely used for the means of trade. I am surprised that a country so far from Europe has developed a similar monetary economy."

Then the chief interpreter said.

"The Japanese currency is forbidden to be taken out of the country. But if you are interested, I will collect some old coins and bring them to you."

Thunberg's interest in coins was so great that in 1779, shortly after his return to his hometown, he gave a lecture on the subject of 'Japanese coins'. The Japanese coins collected in this way, including large and small oval coins, are still carefully preserved in

---

[11] Warlord of the Warring States Period who unified Japan.

Sweden today.

"By the way, Mr. Yoshio I have a favor to ask you."

Thunberg boldly began.

"What is this all about, doctor?"

Kosaku Yoshio asked with a quizzical look on his face.

"I'm talking about the daughter of the nursery man from whom I bought the camellia. Can't I invite her to Dejima and have her take care of the camellias?"

Hearing these words, the chief interpreter was a little taken aback and amazed.

"Taking care of camellias, that it is? I have heard about the girl from Setsu'emon Shige. It is forbidden for town girls to go in and out of Dejima. Of course, if she were Maruyama's courtesan, that would be a different story."

Kosaku Yoshio was lost in thought.

"The magistrate's office would not allow her to live on Dejima, of course. If it is the Doctor's favorite courtesan, then ... but will her father, as well as she, agree?"

6. Journey to the capital Edo

A few more days passed. March 4, 1776, marked the departure for Edo, the biggest event of the year for the Dutch trading factory. Just as the lords of the time would travel to and from Edo on their Shogunate visits, the 'Edo Sanpu' was an annual audience with the Shogun in Edo for the Dutch of Nagasaki to express their gratitude for being granted permission to trade with Japan. It did not mean that the Dutch were trading on an equal footing with Japan, but rather that the Dutch trading factory was still under the control of the Edo shogunate.

The procession of Dutch envoys gathered at Dejima and departed in a solemn manner, being seen off by a large number of people. Only three Dutchmen were among the envoys: the head of the trading factory, the Dutch ambassador Feith, doctor Thunberg, and the secretary Koehler, while the rest, about 60 people, were all Japanese. The Dutch were carried in a black-lacquered palanquin called a 'Norimon'. Soon they passed 'Himi', then 'Yagami', and approached the village of Koga, which Thunberg had seen before. Thunberg opened the small window of the carriage and looked outside. His gaze slid down the rows of people sitting by the roadside, heads bowed, and eventually settled on one girl. Hana was there, too, after all. Thunberg smiled as he gave her a tender look. Hana's hair was adorned with a camellia flower of Thunberg's choice. Hana lifted her head and her eyes met Thunberg's. Their gazes were firmly locked.

"Please be safe on your way."

Hana murmured and watched the Thunberg's palanquin until the group disappeared behind the edge of the mountain.

Most of the Dutch trading factory's cargo, including food, beer, wine, and liqueurs, had been prepared a month in advance and was to be transported by sea to 'Hyogo'[12] via 'Shimonoseki'[13]. However, the goods presented to the Shogun and to other dignitaries of the Shogunate were transported overland, avoiding the risk of damage from storms on the sea route. In Kaempfer's time, it was written that all but the chief of the trading factory rode in rain and cold on horseback; for Thunberg it was comfortable sitting in a palanquin. In the past, Kaempfer had left Nagasaki and traveled by sea along Omura Bay to Sonogi[14], but this trip was made entirely overland.

It had already been eighty-five years since Kaempfer's visit to Edo in 1691. What Thunberg saw was almost the same as what Kaempfer had described. In Europe, this would have been unthinkable.

"In Japan, time does not seem to pass more slowly, it seems to stand still."

Thunberg said to himself.

The group arrived in Kokura[15], in bad weather. They took a ship from there to Shimonoseki and then to Hyogo, where they disembarked and went over a land route to Kanzaki[16]. There, they continued the journey on a small boat to Osaka. At the time, Osaka seemed like a very attractive city to Thunberg.

He hoped to collect many plants on his journey. However, his expectations seemed to have been betrayed at every turn, all the way to Edo. He wrote,

"The fields along the road were so well tended that there was not a weed in sight."

None of the land was fallow or had been abandoned. The only exception was the Hakone[17] mountain crossing. Thunberg got out of his palanquin and walked up the mountain. He planned to try to collect plants here, just as Kaempfer had done. The accompanying interpreters and officials could barely keep up with him as he moved around the mountain nimbly and quickly with a well-trained body from the time in the forest of Africa. Hakone was the only place other than Nagasaki where he could collect plants. Although Thunberg was not allowed to stray far from the travel route at that time, this place satisfied his curiosity about plants.

Finally, on April 27, he arrived in Edo. Since passing through the Ookido in Takanawa[18], more and more townspeople flocked to catch a glimpse of the Dutch delegation.

In the sea of Shinagawa, which could be seen on the right, many vessels loaded with cargo were coming and going. The sight reminded Thunberg of Amsterdam, a city with a thriving commercial center and it made him feel like he had arrived in a big city.

Eventually, Edo Castle began to appear on the left. Rising across the moat, Edo Castle resembled a Dutch water castle, he thought. By the time he reached Nihonbashi[19] Bridge, security policemen were lined up in single rows on both sides of the street, desperately trying to hold back the throngs of people. After crossing the bridge and going a short distance, he saw the bell of Hongokucho[20], telling

---

12   A port of the inland sea, today's Kobe
13   West port of the main island, opposite side of Kyushu Island
14   A small port of Omura Bay
15   A port of Kyushu Island
16   A port near of Osaka, now a part of Osaka city
17   Active volcano (1438m) between Shizuoka and Kanagawa prefecture near of Fuji Mountain
18   A big gate to the capital located at Takanawa town
19   The main bridge of Edo
20   A town area

the time. Turning right at the bell, he found the inn, Nagasakiya.

The Dutch trading factory's permanent lodging house was at the Nagasakiya, the same place where Kaempfer had stayed in the past.

"It is not a fine place to receive visitors from all over Europe."

Thunberg wrote his first impression. The Dutch delegation was not allowed to leave the Nagasakiya freely during their stay in Edo. The entrance was on a back street. The delegation's accommodations were on the first floor, with a private room for the head of the trading factory, a room separated by sliding doors for Thunberg and the secretary, a common dining room and reception room, and a room with a bath and washing facilities. The windows were high up and did not offer a view of the outside world sufficiently.

Feith said:

"A lot of Edo people have been coming in all morning, and we look like showpieces."

Thunberg agreed.

"The children are especially excited when they see our statures through the window. By the way, is there any way to silence the bell that rings every hour?"

"Indeed! There are many churches in Amsterdam, and although I am used to bells, that tone is too low."

The bell of Hongokuho near the Nagasakiya struck without rest in the Kanda neighborhood as if welcoming the Dutch delegation.

The innkeeper, whose name had been Gen'emon Nagasakiya for generations, greeted the group upon their arrival.

"Well, well, Captain Feith, thank you for your long journey. I congratulate you on your safe arrival in Edo. It has been two years since I have seen you, and I am pleased to see that you are in good health. Welcome to Dr. Thunberg, and the secretary, Mr. Koehler. We look forward to working with you."

Gen'emon, who was already familiar with Feith, greeted him smilingly. He was the guarantor of the delegation during their stay in Edo. Having such an important role, he was allowed to accompany the Dutch to Edo Castle. On top of that he was in charge of the custody of the valuable gifts brought by the delegation from Nagasaki to the Shogun and other dignitaries of the Shogunate.

The Dutch delegation waited at the Nagasakiya until they were granted an audience with the Shogun. During this period, many doctors, interpreters, and scholars visited the Dutch. The Shogun's physician, Hoshu Katsuragawa, accompanied by his friend, physician Jun'an Nakagawa, came almost every day. The reputation of Thunberg as a doctor trained in the latest European medicine had already reached Edo. In Edo, Nagasakiya was the only place where the Japanese people, who were both scholars and doctors, were allowed to interact with European civilians.

Gen'nai Hiraga is known to this day as a unique scholar of Dutch study, inventor, painter, and scientist. One day he and Jun'an Nakagawa came to visit Thunberg at Nagasakiya. He had just spent seven years restoring an electrostatic generator 'Elektriciteit', which he had acquired in Nagasaki.

"I have brought it here to show you."

Gen'nai, with his long face, proudly placed the square box in front of Thunberg. He then turned the handle protruding from the side of the box. Soon, a lightning bolt flashed between the two metal bars sticking out of the top of the box like horns.

Thunberg knew about electricity, but his knowledge was not as deep as it should have been.

He did not hide his surprise that a Japanese scientist had repaired such a discharge device. Gen'nai was so pleased that he took something even more interesting out of his bosom. It was a hand mirror with a glass surface plated with mercury. The reflection of his own face on the mirror was a perfect image without any distortion. Jun'an Nakagawa saw it and added,

"The other day, Dr. Thunberg taught us how to treat syphilis using mercury."

Thunberg had learned this remedy when he studied in Paris and which was the most advanced at the time. Gen'nai's knowledge was considerable, and Thunberg could not help but being amazed at his knowledge. The conversation went on talking about tulips.

"The tulips that bloomed from the bulbs given to me by a Captain who came to Edo, were magnificent."

Gen'nai said, and Jun'an added,

"It must have been nine years ago. It was given to you by the Captain named Castens, wasn't it?"

Gen'nai was not only the first person in Japan to make tulips bloom, but he was also a first-class medical herbalist. Thunberg wondered why this genius had a workshop on the street and did not hold a government position. A man as knowledgeable as he would be the perfect person to manage the lord's herb garden. Gen'nai answered without hesitation.

"I really don't want to be tied down in my own whims."

"How do you make a living, then?"

Thunberg asked a somewhat intrusive question.

"I write books, that I do."

It had been a long time since Gen'nai had published his best-selling books, such as 'Nenashigusa'[21] and 'Furyu Shidoken den'[22]. Recently, he had also published a book titled 'Hohiron'[23].

For Thunberg, it was nothing else than a big surprise, that such a genius was living freely inside a country that was closed to the rest of the world.

The Dutch inn, Nagasakiya, attracted a lot of visitors every day. On that day, Genpaku Sugita and Ryotaku Maeno, carrying a copy of 'Kaitai Shinsho'[24], came to the inn with Jun'an Nakagawa. They enthusiastically questioned the book's contents. It was a great surprise and excitement for Thunberg that this book written in Germany had been translated into Dutch and then into Japanese. He showed them the latest surgical instruments he had acquired while studying in Paris and Amsterdam. They were astonished to see the instruments and looked at him with even greater respect for his possessions. He also sold them some of the latest medical books he had brought with him.

There were several earthquakes during his stay in Edo. Sometimes Thunberg himself did not even notice them. But it was the first time he had experienced a building shaking, even though he was not on a ship and there was no wind.

It was not an earthquake, but the great fire in Edo, said Feith, the head of the factory.

"During my first visit to Edo, in the spring of 1772, the fires in Edo were terrible. The fire broke out in the afternoon and burned until the following night, destroying even Nagasakiya, the inn of the Dutch delegation. At that time, we were finally able to settle down in a temple with the townspeople who were running for their lives. It was a very unpleasant experience."

Just then, Gen'emon, the owner of the Nagasakiya, entered the first-floor room with Kosaku Yoshio, the chief interpreter who had accompanied the delegation from Nagasaki, to discuss tomorrow's audience.

[21] Rootless grass
[22] The Story of elegant life of Shidoken
[23] Farting Theory
[24] The New Text on Human Anatomy

"I was just telling Dr. Thunberg about the fire in Edo."
Feith spoke to Gen'emon.
"At the time it was quite a commotion. It was the Great Fire at Meguro Gyoninzaka in year 9 of Meireki era. Fortunately, the goods that were presented to the Shogunate had already been transported to Edo Castle and were saved. However, the fire swept into the Kanda area and finally burned one-third of Edo."
The difficulties of the Nagasakiya, responsible for the accommodation of the Dutch delegation, were hardly imaginable.
"The Dutch trading factory on Dejima was very kind to us on that occasion. It is thanks to you all that we have been able to rebuild the Nagasakiya in such a splendid manner."
Gen'emon bowed deeply to Feith.
The Nagasakiya's main business was the pharmaceutical business, selling medicines brought by Chinese and Dutch ships. In addition to this, it also ran an inn for Dutch delegations visiting Edo, but the house was destroyed in the Great Fire, and rebuilding was not a simple matter. Fortunately, the Dutch trading house sent them sugar, which they were able to sell to finance the reconstruction of the Nagasakiya.
"I heard later that more than 10,000 people died in the fire, and the Shogunate's response was swift and precise."
Feith said, recalling his own experience.
"Temples and residences of feudal lords that escaped the disaster, provided food for the people and many townspeople were saved thanks to the relief huts that sheltered them from the rain and dew."
Nagasakiya Gen'emon, who had experienced the same thing, agreed.
"The Shogun's audience with us was brief because of the emergency situation caused by the fire, and we all returned to Nagasaki immediately. Relief supplies were sent to Edo along the way, and the

Shogunate's leadership in restoring the city was praiseworthy. I was impressed by the Japanese people who waited for help in an orderly fashion without looting the streets of Edo."

Since then, Feith has come to love Japan and the Japanese people, who maintain order in times of crisis without making a fuss.

"Life in Nagasaki can be monotonous and cramped, but I risk it all every other year to come to Nagasaki. I think Japan is worth it."

Never before Thunberg had understood his sentiments. In fact, Feith has come to Nagasaki twice more, to serve as head of commerce.

"It is the bond of the people of Japan, that it is."

Kosaku Yoshio, the chief translator, said in a low voice.

On May 18, the envoys had an audience with Shogun I'eharu. They were dressed in formal attire, armed with swords, and took palanquins from the Nagasakiya to Edo Castle. The Nagasakiya area was filled with townspeople who crowded in to see the Dutchmen.

At Edo Castle, Feith was received by Shogun I'eharu. The offerings brought by the Dutch trading factory were already laid out. Feith, accompanied by the Grand Interpreter, entered the great hall. Nagasakiya Gen'emon is waiting in the next room with Thunberg and Secretary Koehler. Feith moves forward in what he calls a 'crab side-step', bowing flat to the Shogun and the heir to the throne, and then he hears a voice saying "Dutch Captain". Feith can only glance at the faces of the Shogun and the young lord. The head of the trading factory exits with the same motion as before. The curtain falls on a long journey from Nagasaki to Edo.

This was Feith's third time to worship, and he had become quite familiar with the ceremonies. His movements were smooth and the ceremony went without a hitch. In the long history of the worship service, there was also a time when the chief of the trading factory was extremely obese, and it is written that he was 'truly disreputable' at that time.

In the presence of the chief of Roju[25], Okitsugu Tanuma, was also present. This man was a famous politician who brought great prosperity in terms of economy and culture during the An'ei era. He was active in bringing in technology and culture from abroad. Nagasaki, the center of Dutch studies, attracted many young Japanese who were inspired and motivated by his policies.

After the audience, the Dutch representatives move on to the 'Dutch Interview' ceremony. The three members of the trading factory were taken to the White Room in the main palais, where their costumes, hats, and swords were shown to the Shogun, the lords, and the ladies of the palace's ladies chambers. At that time, the nobles who were waiting behind the bamboo screen would ask them various questions.

Shogun I'eharu tended to leave most of the political matters to his liege lord Okitsugu Tanuma and others, while he himself lived in the world of his hobbies. Since Nobunaga Oda[26], shogi[27] has been an accomplishment of feudal lords, and the first Shogun, I'eyasu, was an avid shogi player. It was also I'eyasu who appointed Ohashi Soukei, who served Nobunaga Oda and Hideyoshi Toyotomi, to the Shogi Office. Shogun I'eharu's hobby was shogi, and he himself possessed considerable skill in the game. The Shogun, who had met Feith two years before, suddenly asked him,

"Do you also have shogi in Holland?"

The head of the trading factory was somewhat surprised by the unexpected question, but he calmed down and began to explain about the Western game of chess.

After listening to his explanation, the Shogun was satisfied and said, "I would like to play shogi with the King of The Netherlands someday."

After the audience ceremony, the three delegates were escorted to a tower of Edo Castle, from where they could see the city of Edo in the distance. One of the officials who was accompanying them said, "The city of Edo has a circumference of about 84 kilometers and it takes 21 hours on foot."
The reconstructed town of Edo was a beautiful and harmonious place, accentuated by the endless waves of tiled roofs and the large temple buildings with five-story pagodas that could be seen here and there. It was also a city of water, with canals dug between the rows of houses. Thunberg was impressed with its view and thought it was the most beautiful town he had ever seen. He felt that all the hard work of the long journey had paid off.

In gratitude for the successful conclusion of their audience with the Shogun, the Dutch delegation visited the high officials of the Shogunate in turn, including the Roju, the Wakadoshiyori[28], the Goyonin[29], the Magistrates for Temples and Shrines, the Magistrates for North and South Towns, the Religious Magistrate, and the Magistrate for Nagasaki. The Nagasakiya delivered gifts to each of them in advance. At this time, the streets of Edo were filled with crowds of people who came to see the Dutch delegation, creating quite a commotion.
After these three days of events, on the day before returning to Nagasaki, the Dutch delegation went to Edo Castle again to greet the officials. In front of the dignitaries assembled in the great hall,

---

25	the member of shogun's council of elders
26	A mighty warlord of the Warring States Period
27	Japanese chess
28	Sub-member of shogun's council of elders
29	Representatives of lords

the chief of the religious magistrate read out the 'Gojomoku'. This was a ceremony to confirm the Shogunate policy toward the Dutch. The contents of the articles were the prohibition of Christianity, the continuation of trade with The Netherlands, and the protection of Chinese and Ryukyuan[30] vessels. After the ceremony in the great hall, the Captain retires and receives a gift of ceremonial clothes from the Shogun.

When he returned to his quarters at the Nagasakiya, he also received a return gift from a high-ranking official of the Shogunate.

Gen'emon Nagasakiya came up to greet the three men relaxing on the first floor.

"I thank you all for your hard work. All the ceremonies for this year have now been successfully completed. This year, the Shogun will visit Toshogu Shrine[31] in Nikko next month. Perhaps for this reason, the members of the Shogunate are very busy."

"The journey from Nagasaki to visit Edo is an expensive one, but if the Shogun is moving, I imagine that the expenses will be very high."

As a Dutchman, Feith commented from an economic point of view.

May 25 was the day for the delegation to return to Nagasaki from Edo. A large number of people came to the Nagasakiya to say goodbye. The crowd far exceeded the size of the crowd when the Dutch arrived.

On their return journey, they followed the same route as they had come, taking the Tokaido Route up to the emperor's capital of Kyoto. The return journey was much freer.

In Kyoto, they stayed at the same place as on their onward journey, the Ebiya in Kawaramachi Sanjo, with Bunzo Murakami as the owner. The family business of the Ebiya was the same as that of the Nagasakiya in Edo, and just as the Nagasakiya was in charge of the Dutch delegation's audience with the Shogun, it was in charge of the visit to the Kyoto governor. When the Dutch delegation arrived in Kyoto from Nagasaki, the Governor issued a 'Tokaido Route certificate' for a river crossing by travelers and horses and on their way back to Kyoto, the Dutch delivered a gift as a token of appreciation. On June 12, they were granted an audience at the Governor and also visited the East and West Magistrate's Offices.

"Dr. Thunberg, you have now passed the hurdle of your visit to Edo. You can now relax a little in Kyoto."

Feith said this happily, as if he had something amusing in mind.

"In Edo, I had no time to rest as I had to deal with the scholars who came to visit me every day. I hear we can do a little sightseeing here."

The owner of the Ebiya made the Great Translator explain to Thunberg.

"Tomorrow you will first visit the Hokoji Temple at the foot of Higashiyama mountains. There you will see the largest statue of the Great Buddha in Japan."

The Great Temple was built by Hideyoshi Toyotomi, destroyed by the Keicho earthquake of 1596, and rebuilt by Hideyori Toyotomi. The Great Temple was larger than the one we can see today in Nara, and the floor was covered with white granite. Thunberg was also a harsh critic of the architecture of the Great Temple Hall where the statue sits, saying that it does not get enough light. Twenty-two years after his visit, the Great Buddha was destroyed by lightning and no longer exists today.

"The Sanjusangen-do[32] Hall nearby is also worth a visit."

As the owner of the Ebiya said, the statues of Buddha in this hall

---

30   Southern islands, today's Okinawa
31   Shrine built for the first Shogunn I'eyasu Tokugawa
32   Temple with thirty-three bays, founded 1169 and is known officially as Renge-o-in

were of great interest to Thunberg, and he wrote a detailed account of the various Buddhas in the temple.

He then took a ship from Fushimi down the Yodo River to Osaka. On his return trip, he stayed there for two days, and it was there that he had the most enjoyable part of his journey to Edo. He liked Osaka so much that he compared it to Paris, France.

The delegation stayed at the Nagasakiya Inn in Osaka, where, as in Kyoto, they visited the Governor of Osaka and the East and West magistrates' offices to express their gratitude for the visit to Edo.

After the official ceremonies, the Nagasakiya owner explained the delegation's plans for their stay in Osaka.

"You will visit Sumiyoshi Shrine and Tennoji Temple, as well as visiting a theater. I am a representative of the copper guild, so you will also see 'Fukisho'."

"What exactly is this place?"

"A copper smelter works for export."

"Oh, I see. You mean the copper bars that were loaded onto Dutch ships in Nagasaki? That was a magnificent piece of work. I would like to see it."

"Yes, sir. Let's take a closer look tomorrow. See you then!"

The owner of the Nagasakiya smiled happily.

The play and the dance were not very interesting to Thunberg. He was much more interested in the alleyways lined with bird stores and the gardens with their rare plants. There he bought as many potted plants as he could with money entrusted to him by philanthropists in Amsterdam, money that had of course been spent on his way to Japan, but which he had enough on hand from his private business in Edo.

His purchases there reminded him of the nursery in Koga, on the outskirts of Nagasaki.

"I wonder how Hana is doing now. I wonder if that camellia is still blooming."

Muttering to himself, he walked around looking at the beautifully tended plants. He picked out a maple and a cycad. Thunberg ordered the plants to be packed and sent by sea to Nagasaki. When he returned from Japan, he intended to bring the plants, along with the camellias from Nagasaki, to Professor Burman in Holland.

On the other hand, the copper smelter works called 'Fukisho' attracted his great interest. Copper bars exported from Japan were a highly pure and valuable commodity. Thunberg wanted to know how the copper bars were made, so he went to the smelter and observed every step of the process.

From Osaka, where there was no end of things to see and do, he reached Hyogo, from where he once again traveled by sea to Shimonoseki. The return trip by ship was much smoother than the outbound trip, and he arrived in Shimonoseki within a few days. From there, he crossed over to Kokura, retraced his steps, and returned safely to Nagasaki on June 30. It was the only precious experience in the world during the almost four-month journey.

After returning to Nagasaki, Thunberg again asked the magistrate to allow him to collect plants. His main concern was, of course, Hana and the four camellias. His destination was the village of Koga. It was a day when the sun was shining softly through the clouds during the rainy season. The scenery was already dazzlingly green from the early spring, and the call of cuckoo was echoing through the mountains.

Hana was waiting. When Thunberg saw Hana, he smiled at her.

"I'm finally back from Edo. I am so happy to see you again."

He spoke directly to Hana in the Japanese he had learned.

Hana smiled shyly and pointed out to him where the camellias were planted. Thunberg followed her lead.

At first sight of the camellias, he was relieved. The camellias seemed to have grown a lot after not seeing them for a while.

"Oh, thank you, I'm very happy to see them here."

Thunberg said cheerfully while holding Hana's hand. She also looked happy.

"I have to move these camellias to Dejima now. Will you come with me to Dejima?"

He boldly asked Hana. Setsu'emon Shige, who had accompanied him this time, translated for him and dared to add something that bothered him.

"You know that Dejima is off limits to women, don't you? Agreeing to his offer would mean Maruyama's courtesan, is that correct?"

"……"

Hana nodded with a blush on her face, though no words were heard as she remained silent.

A little more than a month passed. The news of Hana's arrival on Dejima had made Thunberg restless from morning. Setsu'emon Shige had also arrived, and he was waiting for the arrival of the camellias.

The maple and the cycad obtained in Osaka had arrived safely in Nagasaki, and with the approval of the magistrate's office, they had been temporarily placed in the green area of Dejima.

In the afternoon, the long-awaited camellias arrived on a cart. Thunberg and Setsu'emon immediately had them placed in the green on the east side of Dejima.

Thunberg said to Setsu'emon,

"I feel relieved now. I have fulfilled half of Professor Burman's promise. All that remains now is to get the camellias safely to

Amsterdam. I hope they will arrive undamaged."

The two men returned to the Dutch surgeon's house and over a cup of tea talked about the camellias' upcoming voyage.

"Doctor, will you be returning to Amsterdam immediately from Japan via Batavia?"

"That depends on the sailing route, but I might make a stopover along the way. Since I have come all the way to Japan, I would like to stop at a place where I can walk around freely on the way back."

"Do you intend to keep the plants you have collected at that time?"

"No, I will send the precious plants from Batavia to Amsterdam on the first ship that arrives there."

Setsu'emon understood.

"It is a long and arduous journey for Japanese plants through the tropics, that it is."

As dusk approached, news came that courtesans had arrived at the front gate.

"Well, I shall leave now."

Setsu'emon took the opportunity to get his act together and quickly disappeared.

Thunberg followed him outside and looked toward the front gate. Many Dutchmen had already come out, and were waiting for their courtesans to cross the wooden bridge over the island.

Among them, Hana, dressed in the same crimson costume as the camellia, was the last to appear. It was the most bewitching Hana that Thunberg had ever seen. It was as if the incarnation of the camellia had appeared.

The Captain, Feith, found him staring at her in a daze and chilled him.

"Dr. Thunberg, I am amazed that you, a strait-laced person, could find such a beautiful courtesan. You are a great plant collector."

That night, the stars streaked across the sky above Dejima, trailing long tails of stars.

The usually bleak Surgical Dutch house suddenly seemed to brighten up just by Hana's presence. They were talking in his workroom, which was lined with medical instruments and botanical specimens. On the desk were small branches of camellia. He wanted to ask Hana something. It was about how to grow camellias and their seeds.

"It is normal to propagate camellias from seeds, especially when you want to make new flowers. But if you want to grow a lot of the same camellia, you can take cuttings."

She picked up a pair of scissors and cut off a small branch of the camellia. Next, she cut off the bud at its tip. She then cut off half of the lowest leaves and finally cut off the lower tip of the twig at a sharp angle.

"You will soak the twig in water before transferring it to a well-drained nursery."

Thunberg pointed out to her that camellias were bearing young fruits.

She told him further how to get camellia oil and what to do with it. He used all of his Japanese knowledge to understand what she told him.

One month later, on July 31, the Dutch East India Company's sailing ship 'Zeeduyn' from Batavia arrived. Two days later, the flagship 'Stavenisse' arrived with the new head of the factory Durkoop on board. The same procedure as last year was used to inspect the cargo by officials of the magistrate's office, followed by unloading and loading of Japanese goods. In addition to the plants purchased in Osaka, Thunberg also brought in four camellias from

Nagasaki. These plants were in good condition and would survive the long voyage to the other side of the world.

As the day of departure approached, Thunberg felt the pain of saying goodbye to Hana. Then something unexpected happened. The new head of the trading factory asked Thunberg to stay in Nagasaki for one more year. The doctor who had come with him was unreliable. Thunberg's heart was pounding wildly hearing this. He was now attracted to Hana and wanted to stay with her, and it was no longer painful for him to spend another year in Nagasaki. He could have stayed in Nagasaki forever as long as he was with Hana.

The beauty of camellias is no less than that of roses. Roses bloom in summer and give off a mellow fragrance. Camellias, however, are winter flowers. If camellia flowers had fragrance like roses, he might have stayed in Nagasaki.

In his mind, the great force that had been pushing him ever since he left his hometown commanded him to return. That force kept pushing him back, with or without saying so. The new director of the trading factory also continued to hold him back, but there was a limit to what he could do.

Before returning to his country, Kosaku Yoshio, the Great Translator, came to Dejima with a group of interpreters who had been friends of Thunberg. Without any interpreters they could communicate swiftly with each other.

"I have successfully completed my short time of service in Japan. It is with a heavy heart that I must leave Japan."

After Thunberg finished his speech, Kosaku Yoshio, representing the entire group, said,

"Every year, we continue to have exchanges with people from Holland at Dejima. However, there were few years that have been as academically successful as this one, that, I am sure off. This is the result of the learned doctor's virtue. Would you like to keep in touch with us by letter?"

"That's what I'd like as well. I have no definite plans for the future, but when I arrive in Europe and get settled, I will write you a letter. It will be delivered on the ship next year, or the year after at the latest."

"Thank you very much."

They all said in unison.

After the party was over, Thunberg escorted them back to the front gate. At the end, he shook hands with Kosaku Yoshio and said, "Mr. Yoshio, as for Hana ..."

"I understand your concern, Doctor."

"What will happen to her?"

"The girl is only in love with you, so she will probably return to her village. I will speak well of this to Setsu'emon Shige."

Hearing this, his heart felt a little lighter.

On November 23, Thunberg boarded the 'Stavenisse', which was anchored at Takabokojima. Together with the 'Zeeduyn', which had preceded them, they left Nagasaki on December 3.

Standing at the stern of the ship, Thunberg continued to wave to the shrinking town of Nagasaki. Feith, who was watching the situation, approached and asked him.

"Why don't you come to Nagasaki with me again next year?"

He did not answer, but continued to wave his hand at the distant city of Nagasaki and at Hana standing in the port.

On January 4, 1777, the ships arrived safely in Batavia. He decided to stay here for about six months to research the flora of Java. Although his body was light after being released from the restraints of his previous life, his heart was heavy as he remembered Hana. However, the tropical climate here was not easy. Of the 13 people who had celebrated his departure for Japan with a farewell party a year earlier, 11 had already passed away. Until then, his strong body had been disease-free except for lead poisoning. This time he had finally been stricken with malaria. But he was able to recover his health in a short time because of using cinchona bark.

The governor, seeing this, repeatedly invited him to stay on as a doctor in Batavia under favorable terms. But his decision to return to his homeland remained unchanged. Tropical plants certainly have a mysterious and magical appeal. They are different from those back home, where the air is cooler, and from those in the temperate zones of Japan and South Africa. To study its mysteries is to open up a whole field of study. Thunberg was well aware of this. But now it was more important to report to Professor Linnaeus, who is waiting for him back home, the knowledge he had gained and the accomplishments he had achieved. His mind remained unchanged.

7. Whereabouts of the Camellias

What happened to the camellias brought from Japan? On his way back to Holland, Thunberg decided to visit Ceylon and make an exploratory trip there. He had never lost his interest in the island of Ceylon, where once Kaempfer had been. He intended to conduct a botanical survey in Java first. Therefore, the four camellias left Batavia on the East India Company's sailing ship bound for Amsterdam, one step ahead of him.

The camellias arrived in Holland in the autumn of 1777. The news that large packages of the East India Company arrived at the port reached Professor Burman.

He was already seventy-one years old and retired at the time. He also had read the letter that Thunberg had sent to Nicholas upon his arrival in Nagasaki, and he imagined that he would already be on his way home from Japan. If he stayed in Nagasaki for another year, he had no doubt that the camellias he had entrusted to him would be delivered as he had hoped. Then came the news from the Company.

"It is definitely a shipment from Thunberg. I must go there at once."
The old professor said to his son Nicholas, who had already succeeded him.

"No need to go, father, I'll go and take a look."
Professor Burman restrained him with his hand and said firmly,
"I'll go and see what's going on."

He was in a state of excitement that was not typical for him.
"Nicholas, I'm going to be busy. I want four nurserymen immediately.

Have them prepared to go to London, Hanover, Dresden, and Vienna, respectively."

Nicholas looked bewildered.

"What is this all about, father?"

"I can't tell you why. I have to write letters as soon as possible."

With that, the professor hurriedly disappeared into his study. The old wife, who had seen him every day as an old man who could hardly walk, was surprised by his sudden change.

A few days later, Professor Burman and his son accompanied four emissaries to the port. There they saw four camellias, a cycad, a maple, and other plants that Thunberg had purchased in Japan. The old professor must have been very moved. There was nothing wrong with all the plants. He instructed immediately to send all but the four camellias to the botanical garden in Amsterdam.

What the four camellias was concerned, this time they were all taken to various destinations in Europe by a messenger with a letter. They were shipped to the nursery of Mr. Loddiges in Londen, to the Palace Herrenhausen in Hanover, to the Pillnitz castle garden in Dresden and to Schönbrunn Palace in Vienna.

To the most distant destination, Vienna, the transport of a camellia happened by ship, from the mouth of the Rhine River in Rotterdam to Frankfurt, Germany, and from there up the Main River to the ancient city of Bamberg. Then, a horse-drawn carriage took it overland about 130 kilometers to Kelheim, to the bank of the Danube River. From there, the camellia was again put on a ship and traveled up the Danube to Vienna, which was the longest journey.

What happened to the camellia sent to Pillnitz? The camellia was loaded onto a Dutch sailing ship, which entered the Elbe River at Cuxhaven in Germany, then the plant was transferred to a smaller ship in Hamburg, and transported directly to the quay of the

Pillnitz Palace near Dresden. It was planted in a Japanese barrel. The news about the arrival of a camellia from Japan was immediately sent to the court in Dresden. When hearing this, the joy of the king, Friedrich August III, was extraordinary. Immediately, he hurried to the Pillnitz Palace in a carriage together with the Dutch envoy based in Dresden. Gottfried Terscheck, the court gardener, met them at the palace with the camellia. In those days, the court gardener's job was to maintain the gardens, provide fresh fruits and vegetables for the court table, and decorate the various rooms with flowers and plants. It was an extremely important role in maintaining and enhancing the prestige of the court, and thus of the kingdom. The position of court gardener was often hereditary, passed down from parent to child, but the best ones were in great demand. Terscheck had two sons. The eldest son, John Mathew, was following a training in Holland to become a gardener.

Friedrich August III, who had a great interest in gardening himself, saw a lovely camellia and touched its leaves and twigs as if he was handling a great treasure.

"What a tender camellia! It has come all the way across three oceans. I'm amazed it reached this land. It's a miracle how it got here! Will it grow and blossom?"

The king asked Terscheck.

"I will take good care of it and make it bloom beautifully; it will certainly please the human eye for generations to come."

He replied confidently.

The camellia was placed in the orangery. This was the palace greenhouse, so to speak, for plants that thrive in warm climates.

A few months passed. The camellia was in good condition, as if it was not tired of coming from the other side of the world.

And in the still dark winter days of Pillnitz's palace, the beautiful red flowers bloomed, as if to herald the arrival of spring. When the king received the news from Terscheck, he rushed to the palace of Pillnitz to see the flowers. Next came noblemen from the court, and the Count Camillo Marcolini, president of the Royal Meissen Ceramics Company, accompanied by a painter. The camellia sometimes appeared to them as a jewel sent from Japan, at other times it looked like a dainty dancing princess.

The dream of the King of Saxony, many years ago, had finally come true. People gazed at the flowers all day long. A grand spring banquet was held. Needless to say, the centerpiece was the camellia from Nagasaki. A large Meissen plate in the hall of the palace was decorated with a magnificent camellia flower.

This was the first step in Dresden's history as one of the leading camellias cultivating city in Germany. Camellias were eventually exported to other countries, and it became customary for the Russian court to display camellias at balls held around the time of the camellia blossom. By the nineteenth century, the camellia was booming in Europe, providing numerous motifs for literature, music, and paintings.

The camellia was carefully nurtured and gradually grew. According its growth, it was planted in larger and larger wooden pots, but the plant had become too big. In May of 1801, after the camellia of Nagasaki had finished blooming, Terscheck finally decided to plant it in the greenhouse of the court garden. In spring, the wooden exterior walls and windows of this greenhouse were removed, and in autumn they were covered again. The wooden exterior walls were double-layered and filled with leaves as insulation. In the winter, two stoves were placed in the adjoining outbuilding. Heated air was supplied from there to protect the plant from the cold. In the greenhouse figs and other tropical plants were planted. The dimensions of the greenhouse were eight meters by ten meters and the heating hut was two square meters. Carl Adolph, the nineteen year old second son of the court gardener Terscheck, was already working as an apprentice and helped with the replanting of this camellia.

It is not known when this camellia was given its own greenhouse. A book written by August von Minkwitz in 1893 states,

"In recent years a greenhouse has been built exclusively for this camellia, and all spring visitors are delighted by its blossom."

At around 6:00 a.m. on January 3, 1905, a fire broke out in the heating hut of the greenhouse where the camellia was planted. The fire destroyed the roof of the greenhouse, but did not completely burn the camellia inside. The water sprayed by the gardeners who rushed to extinguish the fire quickly froze, which covered the camellia with a coat of ice. Nevertheless, the damage to the camellia was extensive. Burnt branches were cut down, and those that were left to heal from their wounds were further shortened. One can only imagine the grief of the people. Even though the memory of the origin of the exotic camellia, which had come to this area over a hundred years ago, had faded, the camellia that had been passed down from the great-grandfather's generation had been severely damaged. The grief of the gardeners was immeasurable.

But the life of this camellia was strong. In spring, young buds sprouted from its burnt branches, and in summer it was again covered with a coat of green. The following year, the camellia once again blossomed magnificently.

It had seen the Napoleonic War like the two world wars of the twentieth century. It was in 1951 that the wooden greenhouse, built every winter, was renovated. A new dodecagonal greenhouse was built at a cost of 48,000 Deutsche Mark. The windows reached from the floor to the roof, and the pipes that supplied hot water were used directly as the structure of the greenhouse. In the summer, only the outer walls were removed and the hot water pipes were left in place, giving the impression that the camellia was in a huge cage. The present movable glasshouse was completed in 1992, two years later after the wall of Berlin fell. Now the camellia blossoms in a new world, in a world where the paradigm has changed.

The current camellia is 8.9 meters high, diameter of the projected area is 11 meters and it has a trunk circumference of 2.19 meters near the ground.

One wonders what has become of the camellia sent to London. The following relates to the whereabouts at Royal Kew Gardens.

'There is no record of Thunberg sending any plants to Kew Gardens. It is known that he stayed in Japan in 1775-76 and sent plants and seeds to Sweden and Holland. It is true that he stopped in England on his way back to Sweden in 1779 to see the material Kaempfer had brought. If he brought plants to Kew Gardens, they should have been recorded.'

What about the Gardens of Schönbrunn Palace in Vienna?

'Nobody found a record of Thunberg sending camellias there at all. The last war destroyed all the greenhouses and only a few plants survived.'

Finally, there is the Herrenhausen Garden in Hanover.

There is a legend that most of the plants from the 1930s were there around 1880. Unfortunately, there is no record of what the plants were like a hundred years earlier.

After a six-month stay in Batavia, Thunberg left for Ceylon, arriving in Colombo on July 29, 1777. He stayed in Ceylon for another six months until February 1778, where he also went on an exploratory trip. He left there and arrived at the Governor-General of the Cape in South Africa on April 27, 1778. A letter from the university in his hometown awaited him there.

'You are appointed as an assistant professor in the Botanical Gardens of the Uppsala University.'

This meant succession to the position of Professor Linnaeus's son. It was a happy but also a sad news. His mentor, Professor Linnaeus, had passed away on January 10, 1778. Just before his death, his son had succeeded him as professor of botany and medicine at the Uppsala University. The return of the heart is like an arrow. Thunberg left for Europe on the next ship and reached his homeland on May 15.

He never dreamed that another disaster would await him at the end of his long journey. The East India Company's sailing ship on which he was sailing had encountered a huge storm in the North Sea, just a stone's throw from Holland. The precious plants he had collected in Ceylon, that were on deck, were swept away, and Thunberg barely made it to the port of Amsterdam. He was lucky that only the valuable items he had collected in Japan survived.

It was October 1 when he arrived at the port of Amsterdam. It was actually eight years and two months after his departure from Uppsala in August 1770.

Professor Burman and his son were waiting for him in Amsterdam. How moving it must have been to see them again. The cycad and maple he had sent earlier had already been planted in the botanical garden. Professor Burman also told him that the four camellias had been safely sent to their destination. Of course, Hana secretly remained deep in Thunberg's heart.

Professor Burman said:

"Dr. Thunberg, you can speak Dutch freely. Furthermore, you have survived an unprecedented expedition. Will you be a professor at the University of Leiden, and will you be able to teach the younger generation?"

"Professor Burman, you and Nicholas have given me endless support. I can never thank you enough. But I would like to return to my hometown, Uppsala. First of all, I would like to visit the grave of Professor Linnaeus, who sent me away."

He felt very hard to part, though he moved on to London. He visited the German explorer and scholar Johann Reinhold Forster and Joseph Banks, who had been friends with Professor Linnaeus. Banks was a botanist and naturalist who explored the Newfoundland and Labrador region on the east coast of Canada and published a book of the plants and animals he collected according to Linnaean taxonomy. He later joined James Cook's expedition to the South Pacific, where he made great achievements, and was a well-known figure in England.

"Sir Banks, I have a favor to ask of you. I went to Japan and came back safely thanks to the great forerunner, Dr. Kaempfer. I heard that the British Museum has his precious materials in storage. Would it be possible for me to see them?"

"Dr. Thunberg, I understand. I would very much like to take a look at them with you. Perhaps you can explain its value to me in detail."

Banks immediately took him to the British Museum. He was able to take a look at Kaempfer's notes and other collected items stored there. The materials, which had lain dormant in the museum for many years, now spoke vividly to Thunberg. It was as if Kaempfer himself was speaking to them. He shed tears as he recalled his own experiences while looking at the objects left behind by his predecessors who had also traveled to Japan.

He visited Kew Gardens, too, where he was reunited with the

camellia from Nagasaki.

It was also a reunion with Hana's alter ego whom he left behind in Nagasaki. The camellia was still in beautiful bloom, and seemed ready to speak to him at any moment.

However, this meeting with the camellia was ostensibly kept secret because it was never made public that he had sent it. The camellia was the property of George III. The camellia he saw was the only one of the four. Since his return to Europe, Thunberg has not visited any other locations except of London for camellias sent from Japan.

When he visited London, he must have been greatly admired as the hero of an adventurous journey that lasted eight years. His visit to the Kew Botanical Gardens, with its collection of plants from all over the world, would have further enhanced the prestige of Kew Botanical Gardens. Later, this visit was probably the source of the legend that 'the Pillnitz's camellia was sent from Kew Gardens in London'.

When future generations talk about the camellias associated with Thunberg, it is not difficult to imagine the various additions and adaptations that were made in connection with the Kew Botanical Gardens. Thunberg himself may have been less interested in the route his camellias took to their respective destinations. In his mind, Hana was always with him.

On January 30, 1779, Thunberg left London for The Netherlands. There he received the news of the death of Professor Burman. The great benefactor, who had vigorously assisted Thunberg in his adventurous travels, had passed away on January 29. Prof. Linnaeus was also gone, and Thunberg, who had lost a great source of emotional support, stood in the cold rain at the grave of Prof. Burman and wept as he recalled the hardships of his long journey.

He returned to Uppsala at the end of March 14, 1779, via Germany.

He had hardly ever left the city, perhaps in reaction to his previous extensive travels, and his most distant trip was to Stockholm.

After the death of Professor Linnaeus's son, he was appointed professor of botany and medicine at Uppsala University in 1784. Later he was elected rector, and his name has been associated with the university during a long time. In 1802, he was invited to become a professor of botany at the Academy of Sciences in St. Petersburg, Russia, but he never left Uppsala for the rest of his life.

It should be mentioned that after his tumultuous travels he married Birgitta in 1784 at the age of 42, five years after his return from his great adventure. They did not marry right away, or rather, he could not marry because he needed time for the image of Hana to fade away in his mind. No children were born to them. It is said that they adopted a son and a daughter from relatives and fostered another boy from their family.

Birgitta passed away in 1813, and Thunberg died fifteen years later, on August 8, 1828, at the age of 85, in his villa near Uppsala.

The Dutch East India Company began its decline around the time of Thunberg's Grand Tour. In 1780, the company fell into heavy losses, and on December 31, 1799, the curtain finally came down on its one hundred and ninety-seven-year history.

Epilogue

The sacred Mt. Fuji was covered with snow as I looked out the window of ANA Flight 663 when it took off from Haneda. After following the long journey Thunberg had made, I finally headed for Nagasaki. I felt I had to go there one last time.

As I got off the plane at Nagasaki Airport and made my way to Dejima, the mountains, bathing in spring sunlight, greeted me in their pale green garb. Camellias were blooming in the gardens of houses. It must have been on this day that Thunberg left for Edo 236 years ago.

 Dejima, which was reclaimed in the Meiji era (1868-1912) and which lost all trace of its original appearance, is being restored again, although the south side where the front gate used to be is reduced in size. Visitors enter from the southeast entrance, which is now connected to the land. Unfortunately, the Dutch surgeon's residence where Thunberg lived at that time has not been restored. However, the building in which the Captain lived is sufficient to show what it was like in those days.

This building, called the 'Captain's room', has an entrance with stairs going up from both sides, similar to a drawbridge over a Dutch canal. This design, which is strange for a Japanese residence, is said to have been designed by the Dutch who lived on Dejima. Climbing the stairs, I entered a large hall. The hall is a reconstructed exhibit of a banquet to which the Nagasaki Magistrate's Office and other influential people were invited.

I tried to imagine the banquet at the time Mr. Feith and Dr. Thunberg were seated. I wondered how the Japanese who were invited to the banquet must have felt when they were joining the dinner.

Unlike Chinese or French cuisine, even today it is not easy to envision Dutch food. However, the banquet dishes on display here are quite impressive. It is the kind of sumptuous food one would expect to find at a first-class hotel party. People at that time must have been surprised to see how different the food in front of them was from what they were used to, and they must have hesitated to start eating.

After leaving the house of the Captain, I walked along the waterway on the south side of Dejima. I found 'the Kaempfer-Thunberg Monument', erected by von Siebold, who later came to Japan as a doctor. It is inscribed in Latin as follows:

Kaempfer,
Thunberg,
Behold your plants, year after year, green and blooming
And your plants recall proprietors who planted them and are becoming hairs of flowers which, you loved.
Dr. von Siebold.

Perhaps von Siebold was aware of the history of the camellia in Pillnitz. He was born in Würzburg, Germany. He may have visited the camellia in Pillnitz, and the words may have come to his mind at that time. I looked up and saw a camellia tree on the other side of my gaze.

At that moment, I heard a young woman's voice from behind me.
"You've finally come, haven't you?"
I turned around and sure enough, there she was standing.
"Ah, you must be the lady I met in front of the camellia tree in the

Pillnitz Garden."

I couldn't help but shout out loud.

She stared at me with the same big, dark, kind eyes she had then.

The gap of more than two hundred years between Dejima Island and Pillnitz Garden, time and space merged and flowed into one another. Where in the world am I?

"I was sure you would come here."

I had no words to say other than to stare at her muttering, it was true that I was in Nagasaki, at the end of a long journey through the history of the camellia in the Pillnitz Garden and the journey of Thunberg.

I pictured the large camellia of the Pillnitz Garden. I was sure that it would be in full bloom in the greenhouse by now.

Before I knew it, I found myself standing under the large camellia tree. The ground was covered with a carpet of camellia flowers. It was as if I was in a large camellia forest.

The next moment, there was a gust of wind. The wind shook the leaves of the camellia. The wind made the camellia flowers fly up into the air.

How much time had passed?

Before I realised, she had vanished without a sound.

I looked up and saw a crane soaring in the sky.

It was like the figure of a celestial maiden dancing in the sky in the Yokyoku[33] 'Hagoromo'.

A dance music of the East,
Or the green robe in the sky,
Or the garment of the springtime haze,
How charming is the maiden, even the hem of her dress,
The left and right, the right and left, the swing of the flower robe,
the sleeves of the dance, they flutter back and forth.

The crane drew a large circle in the sky, and then danced leisurely across the sky.

It was lost in the haze of heaven.

---

33 A song part of Noh-Theater (mask-play) in Japan

Postscript

How an impressive old camellia tree in the park of Pillnitz castle took us back in history. The author's fascination for a more than 200-year-old camellia tree, brought him to the idea to make a study about some 18th century botanic researchers, who sent camellias from the east to the west, on the ships of the Dutch East-India company.

In different chapters, the life and travels of Carl Linnaeus, Johannes Burman, Engelbert Kaempfer and Karl Peter Thunberg have been described, in a way that the reader is also going back in time and has the impression of accompanying these scientists while standing by their side listening to their conversations.

The book is a pleasure to read and at the same time it is an educational work about the discovery of camellias and the long journey they had to make to finally arrive in good condition on the other side of the world. It is because of these early imported camellias that later on some kings in Germany, the U.K. and Belgium developed an interest and encouraged cultivators to import more of them.

Should this book not trigger you to dig a little deeper to learn more about camellias and their history, it for sure will make you look differently at these beautiful flowers in your garden or on the terrace. They might even inspire you to find out more about the first scientists with interest in camellias, their live and their discovery period in Japan, long time ago.

I have enjoyed reading this book and I hope you have enjoyed it equally as much.

Frieda Delvaux

References

1. **Dutch studies in Kyushu, Cross-border and exchange**
   W.Michel, Yumiko Torii, Mahito Kawashima, collaboration, Shibunkaku Publisher

2. **Audience trip to Edo**
   C.P.Thunberg, translated by Fumi Takahashi, Heibonsha Co.

3. **Dutch East India Company**
   Akira Nagatsumi, Kodansha Co. Gakujutsubunko

4. **East India Company**
   Minoru Asada, Kodansha Co. Gendai Shinsho

5. **Kaempfer and Burnie Festival**
   Association Kaempfer and Burnie, Kanagawa Newspaper Co.

6. **Empire Hapsburg**
   Masahiko Kato, Kawade Shobo Shinsha Co.

7. **Sixty articles to know South Africa**
   Yoichi Mine, Akashi Sobo Publisher

8. **Der grosse Bildatlas zur Weltgeschichte**
   Unipart Verlag Stuttgart

9. **Das Geheim der Kamelie**
   Mustafa Haikel, Sandstein Verlag Dresden

10. **Der Kamelienwald**
    Mustafa Haikel, Sandstein Verlag Dresden

11. **Kaross und Kimono**
    Carl Jung, Franz Steiner Verlag, Stuttgart

12. **Great English Speech**
    Yoshio Arai, Eikosha Co.

13. Reise durch einen Teil von Europas, Africa und Asien, hauptsaechlich in Japan,
    Carl Peter Thunberg, Heinrich Groskurd, printed in USA

14. Meissener Porzellan von 1710 bis zur Gegenward,
    Stadt Koeln Kunstgewerbemuseum (1983)

15. The time of Okitsugu Tanuma
    Shinzaburo Oishi. Iwanami Shoten

16. Okitsugu Tanuma
    Genzo Murakami, Mainichi Shinbun Co.

17. Dutch in Edo
    Kazuo Katagiri, Chuko Shinsho

18. Carl von Linnaeus
    Tommy Iseskog, translated by Ayuko Uekura, explained by Fumito Mutoh, Tokai University Shuppankai

19. The life of Gen'nai Hiraga
    Imao Hirano, Chikuma Bunko

20. The Garden of remaining blossom, Sleeping Iwane, Edo graphic novel 13
    Yasuhide Saeki, Futaba Bunko

21. History tale: an accident
    Chuji Hiruki, Bungeisha Co.

22. Edo city map
    Jinmonsha Co.

23. Dejima
    Bord of Education, Nagasaki city